SUSAN HILL is the winner of numerous literary prizes, including the Somerset Maugham award. In 2014, she was awarded a CBE for her services to literature. Author of the Simon Serrailler crime series and numerous other novels, her literary memoir *Howards End is on the Landing* and the ghost stories *The Man in the Picture*, *The Small Hand* and *Dolly* are all published by Profile Books. *The Woman in Black* is published by Profile in hardback.

'Traditional ghost stories of wonderful elegance … Hill builds an atmosphere of creepiness in very few words; the pictures she creates in these stories are unforgettable' Kate Saunders, *The Times*

'Hill knows how to chill you to the bone in the most disarming way … This collection digs deep into the human psyche, exploring its hinterland for paranormal disturbance … With consummate artistry, Hill creates stories that prowl around your mind, coming at you from unexpected angles, invading your senses. Perhaps read them out loud to a friend? Advantage: there's safety in numbers.' Imogen Lycett Green, *Daily Mail*

'Susan Hill proves yet again that she really is the master of the supernatural.' Fanny Blake, *Woman and Home*

The
TRAVELLING
BAG

The
TRAVELLING
BAG

And Other Ghostly Stories

SUSAN HILL

P

PROFILE BOOKS

This paperback edition published in 2017

First published in Great Britain in 2016 by
PROFILE BOOKS LTD
3 Holford Yard
Bevin Way
London WC1X 9HD
www.profilebooks.com

1 3 5 7 9 10 8 6 4 2

Typeset in Fournier by MacGuru Ltd

Printed and bound in Great Britain by
CPI Group (UK) Ltd, Croydon CR0 4YY

A CIP catalogue record for this book is available from the British Library.

ISBN 978 1 78125 620 6
eISBN 978 1 78283 237 9

Contents

For my much loved son-in-law,
Jack Ruston

THE
TRAVELLING
BAG

PART ONE

'Tell me, what would you say has been your most — shall we say "intriguing" case, Gilbert?'

Tom Williams and I were sitting over an after-dinner brandy in the small library of our club. It was a dreary London evening, but in here, the fire glowed and the lamps cast circles of tawny light. One or two other members had come and gone but it was the Upper Drawing Room which would be crowded — that and the card rooms. The Great Library was closed while the beautiful old plasterwork, which had been damaged by a leaking roof, was restored.

Tom Williams was a retired bishop, but you would never have known it, for he was without a vestige of the usual smoothness or pomposity too often acquired by his kind and preferred the modest but comfortable surroundings of this club, whose name was not well known, to the grander premises of smart ones. The Tabor was tucked away down a side street of St James's, unimposing, perhaps even a little shabby. But it was efficiently run and had better food than most clubs – a well-kept secret. Some of its members had names to conjure with but those were accompanied by retiring personalities. There were statesmen, members of the judiciary and high-ranking military men, and they all mingled easily with artists, writers and gentlemen of the turf, and even with someone of my profession, if such it can be called.

I am a psychic private investigator. I studied mathematics and philosophy at Cambridge and followed with a second degree in the natural sciences. But from very early on, my deepest and most compelling interests were the investigation of crime, including the psychology of the criminal, together with the extra-sensory powers of the mind. I am not a spiritualist, nor do I dabble in any form of the occult. I do not tout for clients. I have more work than I can comfortably handle and turn down at least half the requests I receive for my services. People know of me, though I have never advertised.

So it was that, over dinner with Tom Williams, I had been answering some of his questions about both aspects of my work, although he was more intrigued about the investigative side, which was understandable, given his Christian profession. In my view, however, the psychic is only an example of the variety of untapped human potential and has nothing to do with any form of religion. On those matters I stand neutral, a respectful sceptic.

'Every case has its fascinating aspect,' I said now, lifting my brandy glass towards the glow of the fire and watching its contents seem to blaze. 'I would not take one on which did not. They have much in common too, yet each is unique in one way or another and it is that which provides the excitement and the challenge.'

'Pluck one out.'

It came to me at once, as these things do. A picture formed in my mind of a downtrodden-looking man and then, superimposed upon it, one of a woman, wearing a violet-coloured coat with a fur collar, and a small hat. Her expression was one of pleading and anxiety but there was also a determination in her face and a singleness of purpose. She had appeared in my consulting rooms without appointment, at the end of a bitter January day and, after I had invited her to sit down, she had leaned forwards in the chair opposite to mine. She held, close to her, an old-fashioned travelling bag of brown, cracked and faded leather.

'I see by the glint in your eye that you have hit upon a case,' Tom said, smiling.

'Yes. Perhaps because it is linked closely to this club. One or two things happened within these walls.'

'Then I will order us another brandy and you will tell me the tale.'

I shook my head. 'No. There is rather too much for the end of a long, convivial evening and I must be up early tomorrow. Besides, I would like to glance again at my case notes first. Let us meet here in a week's time.'

Tom agreed, albeit reluctantly, for I had whetted his appetite, he said, and he was impatient to hear the story. We set up our appointment for the following Wednesday, which is generally a quiet evening in the Tabor – possibly because it is the only evening, other than a Sunday, when the roast meat trolley is not wheeled out.

We parted and as soon as I got home, I dimmed the lamps in my quiet sitting room and sat recalling the story clearly, without any need to consult my old case notes. Once I have begun to focus, a single image is usually enough to lead me to the rest, and I had already recalled one that evening.

I would tell my tale as if I were reading aloud from a book. Tom was the best sort of listener, eager, but quiet and attentive and I knew he would not interrupt me until the story was done.

I happened to have some free evenings – a visit to the opera and two dinners had been cancelled. It was the season of infectious coughs and colds in the city and people were inclined to stop at home. I was able to prepare myself well.

This was my story.

One

When Walter Craig was in his first year as a student of medical science, it was already clear that he had a fine mind, a dedication and an application to his work which would see him go far. But even more important, he had a flair, a spark of inventiveness that gave him the ability to make intuitive connections which others did not see. Although these had then to be put to the test, step by careful step, they were almost always proved to be correct and he obtained a first-class degree with the highest possible marks. He went on to begin ground-breaking research into the workings of the central nervous system, which promised to have important application to the treatment of some devastating diseases. Those who began to make practical use of his theoretical work were awestruck that so young a man should be making such discoveries. A brilliant future surely lay ahead of him, together with all the honours and prizes he would naturally attract.

But he was a shy, modest and even rather nervous man who preferred to spend his time in the laboratory, or at his desk, rather than socialising and otherwise putting himself about. It was left to others, then, to promote his discoveries.

He worked hard – too hard. After six years of intensive study he took a bad cold one winter, and the cold developed into pleurisy and then pneumonia. He was desperate to get back to his work but lacked all energy – both physical and mental – to do so, and sank into a lethargy accompanied by a deep depression which lasted many weeks. Before his illness he had been working on a new theory about the make-up of the spinal cord, in terms of electrical impulses travelling between there and the brain. He had some proof of his theories but needed to do many more painstaking experiments and the fact that he was unable to continue was the greatest frustration he could suffer. There seemed to be nothing else of interest in his life, though he enjoyed listening to choral music and went regularly to hear the college choir, in spite of being no sort of religious believer. Yet there was something spiritual about his response to choral singing and indeed, in one sense, to the discoveries he was making in his work.

In so far as people knew Walter Craig at all, they liked him – for what was there to dislike? Certainly his prolonged absence was noticed – no one else burned the lights so late. But it would be too much to say that he was greatly missed.

When he was ready to come back, his doctor recommended that he obtain some help with the routine parts of his research and, after initial reluctance, he agreed. He realised that, as well as receiving assistance, he would be giving someone else valuable experience. He had never been a teacher, and, until he found exactly the right pupil, he said that he did not know whether he would make a good one. He interviewed five potential assistants and rejected all of them. He gave no reasons, beyond saying either that they were 'not up to it' or that he would be unable to work with them. And then, the sixth applicant appeared. Silas Webb was just the sort of young man that anyone who knew Craig assumed would be rejected out of hand. He was very handsome, had an almost boyish enthusiasm for medical science, and his knowledge of the area Craig worked in was already good. Webb's open and engaging manner concealed a certain slyness and he was not universally trusted, though no one ever put a finger upon why.

After a couple of months, one of the professors asked how Webb was getting on. Craig was thoughtful for a moment – he never made quick replies to questions, let alone passed quick judgement.

'He is sound,' he said. 'He is able and willing. I think I can teach him a good deal, if only he will listen and be patient. He has clever ideas of his own but he does not always follow them through and he lacks that painstaking attention to detail which is vital. But he has taken a lot of the routine work off my shoulders, so that I can devote my energies to new ideas. He still needs supervision – I dare not leave him entirely to his own devices. But without him I should be much further behind, thanks to this wretched illness.'

He was still easily exhausted, no longer had the stamina to work late into the night and occasionally had to take a full day off to rest. He had aged. He had a general greyness about him. But he had recovered all his passion for his work and for making discoveries and he was as excited as ever when some experiment 'came out' or calculations proved correct.

Several months later, when it seemed that his work was reaching a critical point, he was taken ill again, with a recurrence of the old pattern of fever, deep depression and complete exhaustion, and this time his doctor was cautious in his prognosis. Craig would recover but it would take longer and perhaps the after-effects would be lasting. He might return to his work but it seemed likely that he would be prey to these debilitating attacks for the rest of his life.

For two weeks, Silas Webb carried on working alone, arriving early and leaving late. He used the extra time, he said, to pursue some research of his own.

And then he disappeared. He did not come into the laboratories, the science library or the college office. He left no message and replied to none. After a few days, someone went round to his lodgings. The landlady said that he had gone, although his bill was paid up to the end of the term. His rooms were empty of every trace of him.

Walter Craig was told but he was sunk into a deep lethargy and appeared not to be interested, or to care. He would find another assistant when he returned and he said again that, although he had liked Silas well enough, he did not have the finest of minds, the ultimate spark of genius to reach the heights of scientific discovery. 'Though with application he might, perhaps, climb half-way.'

Two

It was a full two years before Craig was well enough to be able to come back without the need to take days off for rest. Gradually, he had grown physically stronger and he returned to the work which had been coming tantalisingly close to fruition. But his mental sharpness was blurred beyond repair. As soon as he tried to pick up old threads he found that he no longer made the instinctive connections which had led him so far along new paths. Realist that he was, he decided that he would go step by small step back over everything, until he arrived again at the point where he had had to break off because of his illness. Perhaps new links and ways forward would present themselves as he worked and he would reach his goal by the careful, methodical process of science.

He had not progressed far before he began to

discover gaps where he had previously joined threads together. Whole sets of figures and calculations were missing. He came to dead ends, and whereas he knew that he had unquestionably progressed to, let us say, Point Eight, the results now before him came to a full stop at Point Five. Vital sections were missing. Piece by piece, day after day, he retraced his steps, once again working far into the night, but to no avail. The conclusions were always the same. In his wilder moments, when he was completely exhausted, he began to doubt himself, to question whether he had really made the progress he imagined, after all. But, in his right mind, he knew that he had.

Walter Craig was a proud and independent man and it was several days before he took his case to a couple of his seniors, but once he had decided to do so, his resolution was firm. The evidence seemed to him as clear as spring water.

His claim was dismissed out of hand.

'You were seriously ill, Craig, your memory failed you – through no fault of your own, I stress, no fault of your own. There appear to be some gaps in this work but there is no evidence whatsoever that anything has been tampered with. You say that the only person who had access to it was Dr Webb, but he disappeared over two years ago and has never raised his head here again, though I believe that he was heard of at one of the German universities, doing interesting work. I know nothing more and I would advise you to draw no conclusions and make no accusations. Take time to pursue some other line of research. Then again, there is teaching a-plenty for you. We have a very promising intake of young scientists who would benefit from your guidance.'

Instead, insulted and proud, Craig took up a post in London, less senior than he merited but which gave him, along with a light teaching load, time to pursue his own work.

He had continued in this way for several years, and was apparently content, until he sat down one evening to read the latest issue of an academic quarterly which covered his own general field. He quickly digested two short articles before coming to the principal section of the journal, which always contained a piece of important original research. To achieve publication here represented one of the highest pinnacles of a career. It would usually lead to opportunities for further research, promotion, and even eventual fame and glory. The work of Nobel Prize winners and Fellows of the Royal Society had on occasion been first noticed in the journal.

Craig settled down to read and as he read, he was at first puzzled, but then greatly shocked, to recognise his own work, his own discoveries and applications. All the essentials were set down on these pages – references to tests, calculations and conclusions made and results anticipated, although, naturally, some significant details were omitted. No one was incautious enough to reveal their full hand to the greedy outside world, and those who were legitimately interested in pursuing the matter would go straight to the author of the paper.

He read on, seeing before him the lost links, the statistics which had apparently vanished, the missing pages. The paper used everything he had spent so many years working out and proving. All the conclusions drawn had been enabled by his missing data. He felt nauseated as he re-read and then misery and a deep sense of both failure and betrayal quickly overcame him. He knew what had happened, of course, the moment he read the name of Dr Silas Webb. He also saw, at the same moment, that he could do nothing. There was no point in protesting to the editors of the journal, or even to Webb himself.

He had no proof, it would be his word against that of a man who had been his assistant and gone on to great success. There was nothing unusual about that. The pupil has often outstripped the master, to reverse roles when that master has nothing more to teach.

He set the journal aside and sat, hunched into his chair, brooding. Anger and bitterness burned slowly inside him and he woke the following morning feeling the weight of far more years than were on the calendar, certain that he would now achieve nothing to mark him out from the herd of mediocre men.

He never spoke about the matter. He did not pursue it. And over the course of the next fifteen years, he looked on at the rise of Silas Webb.

They did not meet. Webb now began to move in illustrious circles. The research led to glory, when it was successfully applied in a clinical context, diseases of the central nervous system were targeted and sufferers given new hope, at first gaining relief and short-term improvement, later, complete cures.

Throughout this time, Walter Craig pursued his own work doggedly, though mechanically, and endured rather than enjoyed his obscure life.

Silas Webb became a Fellow of the Royal Society and a knighthood came to him, as well as a large number of honorary degrees from illustrious universities round the world. But he held no university post himself, and seemed not to be pursuing further research. Rumour had it that he was devoting his energies to an important book. He never acknowledged Craig or referred to the time he had spent under his tutelage.

Craig forgot and forgave nothing, only occasionally allowing himself a bitter outburst against his former pupil when he was by himself, during which he sometimes gave voice to wild threats of revenge.

He was too much alone and had too much time for brooding. But during his early years in London, an old acquaintance had put him up for membership of the Tabor Club, thinking that Craig was a stranger in the place and would enjoy meeting others, including, in all probability, members of his own profession. The man acted more in hope than expectation, knowing Walter as he did, but in fact Craig took to the club and enjoyed quiet evenings dining there alone, sitting over a book, or even engaging in conversation, though he was always more of a listener than a talker and many who sat with him over a late drink were given no idea of his occupation. He was generally taken for a retired lawyer.

He came into the club one evening in time to have a drink over the evening paper, and then dine alone. It was a wet London night and a taxi cab had driven hard through a deep kerbside puddle, splashing his trousers. He paused on the first landing to check that his shoes were not also full of water. Just ahead of him, the door to one of the card rooms had been opened, and left for a moment, by a servant carrying in a laden tray. The room glowed like a tableau, lit from within. Six green baize-topped tables were set out, with four players at each, their faces like those in some old Dutch master, shadowed behind but with their features brilliant in the light. As Craig glanced through the open door, he saw that the man at the nearest table, and immediately opposite him, was Silas Webb. He looked sleeker, ruddier, more prosperous and filled-out than when he had last seen him but it was unmistakeably Webb.

The door closed.

Because he had been looking into the dimness of the landing outside, beyond the card room, the man could not have made him out, Craig reasoned, even if he had not been studying his cards.

Craig had never seen him in the club before and he would surely have done so if Webb had been a full member.

As he climbed the final flight of stairs to the small library, he met the senior steward coming down.

'Good evening, Dr Craig.'

On impulse, Craig stopped him and asked if knew Sir Silas Webb.

'Indeed, yes. In fact he is in the card room now, guest of Lord Mullivan. I could take any message you may have to him, in the game break.'

Craig shrank back, saying that he had merely wanted to check. 'An embarrassment, you know, to mistake a man for another. I don't think I have come across him in the club before.'

'Sir Silas is a guest and staying with us tonight, as the card gentlemen usually play late. As a matter of fact I will be up in a few minutes, to brush out his room.'

Walter's face must have registered surprise that the head steward worked as one of the cleaners, because the man smiled.

'It is not quite what you would understand by "brushing out", sir. Sir Silas has a fear of moths and at this time of year, moths do tend to be about, as you will know, so he likes to have his room inspected and brushed out thoroughly before he retires. We have several domestic staff off tonight with this wretched influenza, so I am happy to oblige.' He lowered his voice, looking conspiratorial. 'With other gentle-man, you know, it is spiders.'

A couple of members came up the stairs towards them and the steward hurried away.

In the small library, having ordered his customary dry sherry, Craig concealed himself behind the evening newspaper and thought about what he had been told. Webb had never shown a fear of anything when he had worked as his assistant, though he had had a horror of chalk screeching on blackboard and would wince if he heard it. But he had never complained or suggested that the use of small blackboards for making quick calculations and then erasing them, be abandoned. Perhaps he felt rather more important now, a man who was confident in ordering that his room should be brushed out before he slept in it. Craig would have sympathised with anyone else who suffered from such phobias but he had nothing but bad feeling towards Webb.

Over his dinner, sitting alone at a corner table, he thought about it to the exclusion of anything else, and when he had finished, instead of returning to the library, he took the lift to the club's top floor, on the west side, in which the dozen guest rooms were situated. All the doors were closed, save for one at the far end, from which light slanted into the corridor and he could hear the soft sound of a brush sweeping slowly to and fro. He looked in and saw the steward patiently moving it up and down the walls, over the furniture and down the curtains. The man glanced up and asked if he could help.

21

'I just came up to see if you would very kindly show me a couple of these guest rooms, Mr Potts? I have an old friend coming up to town who might wish to stay a night, but between us, he is quite particular.'

'You're welcome to see in here, Dr Craig, I have all but finished, and then I can show you Room Eight, which is vacant tonight, and which has a different aspect. When might your friend wish to stay with us, sir? We do become very busy up to Christmas.'

'No, no, it would not be before then. Thank you.'

Craig had stepped into the middle of the room which Silas Webb would occupy that night. It was quite large and though the furnishings were old-fashioned, everything was well appointed and comfortable. An overcoat hung behind the door and a pair of shoes was placed in front of the wardrobe. In the bathroom, he noted that a sponge bag was monogrammed, S.W. Otherwise, there was nothing personal save an old leather travelling bag on the luggage stand, resembling a doctor's Gladstone bag, sturdy and well used.

He suffered the steward to show him round the vacant Room Eight, feigning interest, before he returned to the small library and a glass of brandy. Walter had always avoided thinking about Silas Webb. If he had ever come upon his name in reference to some new honour or award bestowed upon him, he did not allow himself to dwell upon it, knowing that it would only distract him, and embitter him further. He could do nothing, prove nothing. He had much better turn away.

Tonight, however, all the anger and resentment at his own betrayal, and at Silas Webb's rise to the top of the tree, boiled up inside him. He rang for a second brandy, which was something he rarely did, but he needed to calm himself and stop his hands trembling. His life had been blighted and his career set back, by an illness for which no one was to blame. But Webb had taken advantage of his long absences to steal his ideas, theories, proofs, and to remove any traces of vital individual, and possibly identifiable, links, after he did so. Without conscience he had presented the work and findings as his own and been rewarded and lauded for it. He had risen, unjustifiably and without shame, to the top of his profession, on the back of another man.

Craig had never regarded titles and honours as especially desirable and he did not covet money, but he was proud, proud of his work and what good its applications might do. He was deeply angry that someone he regarded as a lesser man had achieved recognition for it.

It grew late. He heard voices on the staircase. If he went out there now he might encounter Webb and he had no wish for a confrontation. As he drank his brandy slowly, he allowed the hint of a plan that had entered his mind to ripen, and his pangs of conscience to weaken, until there was no longer anything between him and his determination. He decided to return to the Tabor the following evening, in the hope of catching the head steward, but, as he left now, he met the steward crossing the front hall.

'Goodnight, Dr Craig.'

'Steward, I know it is late and I am sure that Sir Silas will have retired ...'

'He has not long gone up, sir, but there is still time for me to take a message to him.'

'No, no, I don't wish to have him disturbed, the matter is not urgent, but I wonder – how might I discover when he is staying here next?'

'He is always here as a guest on card nights and you have only to look in the visitor's book on the porter's desk to see if he is staying.'

They parted and Craig found a cab to take him home, nursing both his old hatred and a new-found sense of anticipation.

Three

When the card room door had been left open, Silas Webb had, in fact, caught a glimpse of the man standing on the landing outside. He had not caught Walter Craig's eye but even a second's glance had shown him a changed man. And yet, he had thought as the door swung to, perhaps not essentially changed after all. He had always judged Webb to be a grey man, somewhat messy and downtrodden in appearance, and as he turned his attention back to the card table it occurred to him that, clever though he was, Craig had always been destined for ultimate failure, a man who slipped down rather than climbed up. Webb had buried his own part in that failure and fall so deeply that now he barely acknowledged it to himself, but seeing Walter Craig after so many years peeled away his defences and he felt naked and altogether ashamed. The feeling lasted only seconds and by the time he had bent his head to his hand of cards, he had crushed it.

But Craig's face stayed with him, superimposing itself on those of his fellow players in turn, coming between him and his hand, and following him up to his room in the early hours. He cursed the man, but, as he settled to sleep, he had fully restored his image of himself as a success, and one achieved entirely through his own talent and efforts. If he had not picked up and built upon what he had by now convinced himself were the small beginnings made by Craig, nothing more could possibly have come of them. His own rewards were thoroughly justified.

The small dark worm of shame deep inside him squirmed slightly.

But if he met the man again face to face, he decided that he would acknowledge him.

Four

Several weeks passed, during which Walter Craig made preparations. After that, he had only to wait. He visited the Tabor every night, to dine or to spend an evening in the library, occasionally not to stay but to look in the guestbook. He was a patient man and an unobtrusive one and he drew no one's attention.

On an evening in early December, he saw the notice on the card room door listing the players in a tournament on the following night. He was ready. Nothing had been left to chance. His task had been surprisingly easy, once he had made enquiries and paid a visit to a house in Surrey. He was given careful instructions. Nothing else was needed.

He had anticipated some setback or complication on the night itself, but none had occurred and he began to feel as if his way had been made straight, eased, because he was in the right and his actions justified. Besides, he was merely making a gesture, perhaps a rather foolish one – at worst he was about to play a prank, nothing more. He had never gone in for practical jokes as a boy but on those odd occasions when he had played one and been successful, he had felt a spasm of the purest joy which had borne him up through many wearisome days.

Tonight, as he entered the club and went straight to the side staircase that led to the upper floor and the guest rooms, he was anticipating that same joy, only flavoured now with the exquisite spice of revenge.

PART TWO

Tom Williams had listened intently to my story so far but now I saw that he yawned. The fire had been topped up twice during the previous hour but just then it collapsed into a soft heap of ash. I stood up. 'Come on, Tom, home time. My Lady Bishop will be wondering.'

'No!' he said, 'You cannot simply leave the story dangling there. I demand to hear the rest.'

'Indeed you shall, but another night. I am worn out.'

'Then let it be tomorrow. I will try to exercise my soul in patience until then. But let me have a hint, something to tease me, a titbit to chew on.'

'I am engaged tomorrow, but the next night, you can give me dinner and then we will retire to this same corner and I will tell the rather unpleasant conclusion to my tale.'

Five

The death of Sir Silas Webb was reported in the newspapers the day after it occurred but although there were fulsome references to his eminence, honours and awards, the circumstances and manner of his demise were not mentioned, other than to say that the coroner had recorded it as having been due to 'natural causes'.

In fact, Webb had died of heart failure in a guest room at the Tabor Club some time between ten minutes to two, when he was seen going up to bed at the conclusion of a card game, and seven-fifteen the next morning, when the servant went to wake him with tea. On receiving no reply to his knock, the man entered and found Sir Silas' body on the floor. He was still fully clothed, in dinner dress, though his black tie was undone and hanging loose, as if he had clutched at it desperately to try to get himself more air.

There was a private funeral and a grand memorial service, attended by hundreds of prominent and eminent men, after which the matter, like Sir Silas, rested.

Some three months later I was writing up case notes at the end of the day when there came a soft knock on the door of my consulting room. I was expecting no one. My last client had left at five and it was now gone six. The lamps were lit in the street and the one on my desk shone onto my papers.

I opened the door to a woman of late middle age, dressed in a violet coat with a fur collar, a small violet hat, and neat black buttoned boots. She was carrying a bag.

'Dr Roper? I am sorry to arrive without warning but I do hope that you might be able to see me.'

I explained that my working day was over and that it was usual for prospective clients to make an appointment in advance, but she looked both distressed and determined.

'I understand and I have been on the point of telephoning for some days but every time I have almost done so, I have lost my nerve. It was only by acting on impulse and before I could have second thoughts that I managed to come here today.'

The shoulders of her coat were damp with rain, her face was pale and so wretchedly drawn, with the effects of sleeplessness and worry, that I could not find it in myself to send her away. I indicated a chair and she sat on the edge of it, holding the bag closely to her.

'I am certain that if anyone can help me, if anyone can find out the truth, it is you, Dr Roper.'

'I am flattered, though you may well be wrong. I must ask how you have heard of me.'

'Your name is – known. Friends … people in whom I have confided have told me … I have never seen any form of advertisement.'

'I do not advertise. I have as much work as I can do coming solely from personal recommendation. But – you know who I am. May I please have your name?'

'Hesther Webb. My husband – my late husband – was Sir Silas Webb. Perhaps you may have heard of him?'

'I have and please accept my sympathy, Lady Webb.'

She inclined her head slightly.

'I am not sure how … what …' She looked down at her hands which were fidgeting with the gloves she had removed. I waited. She looked up at me, pleading in her eyes.

'Perhaps it would help if I told you how I work?'

'Thank you. Yes.' I could barely hear her.

'It depends on what exactly it is that you want, what the case concerns and how complex. For example, if a member of your family had gone missing …'

'I need you to find out the truth about my husband's death. It was decided quickly that he had died of sudden heart failure – you may know that the Coroner set it down as that. But he had no history of heart weakness and he had not been ill recently, in any way. My husband was rarely ill and never seriously so in the fifteen years I knew him.'

'Nevertheless,' I said, as gently as I could, 'it is perfectly possible for the heart to fail without warning and without any apparent history.'

'But it feels wrong, so very wrong. I am certain that something happened to him, something which caused his unnatural death.'

'What sort of thing?'

'That is just the problem, Dr Roper. I have no idea. I am just as sure as I can be that all was not as it seemed.'

'Are you suggesting that your husband died by – I must speak bluntly – that someone killed him? For that is the only possible explanation for his death, other than natural causes, suicide or accident. Suicide was ruled out, even had he any reason, and so was accident – for example if he had fallen and hit his head – there would have been immediate evidence of that, which would have been picked up by the police and the first examining doctor.'

'And they found nothing. There were no signs of anything like that having taken place.'

'If his death was caused by someone else – I speak bluntly again – only in the realms of fiction is it possible to kill another person and leave no trace. Even poison betrays itself. I am sure you have thought about all this, Lady Webb.'

'I have thought of nothing else, night and day, since my husband died.'

'Did Sir Silas have any enemies?'

'Every man who achieves the worldly success and recognition he did must surely attract some dislike … but deadly enemies? No, of course not. No one would have wished him harm, I am quite certain of it.'

'Then …?'

'I have nothing to base my suspicions on. No evidence. Nothing other than an inner conviction.'

'I understand, and our inner convictions are always to be taken seriously, but what would you wish me to do? Others in their official capacity have investigated your husband's death most thoroughly and I would not dream of casting doubt on the findings of honest professional men.'

'I have heard that … that you have some remarkable powers. I do not fully understand what they are.'

'I am not a spiritualist medium, Lady Webb, if that is what you have been told. I do not contact the dead, nor ever claim or pretend that I do. But sometimes I am given a view into the past – in a series of scenes that come to my mind. These are scenes of events that have taken place in the past, sometimes recent, sometimes more distant, but which I can see again. It is not easy to explain – indeed, I do not really understand it myself. I do not mean that I am able to conjure up past events in which we have been involved, in memory. We can all do that. What I see is something I have not experienced myself.'

'So – you could somehow see what happened to my husband, see it happening? You …'

I raised my hand. 'I can only try. And often I fail. I offer no guarantees.'

'But you will try? Please tell me that you will try. Whatever you require, money, yes, of course, I will pay whatever you ask, now.'

'I do not ask for any payment, Lady Webb. I have the good fortune to be a man of private means. I work because I am sometimes able to help others. I could never be idle. All I need is an object that belonged to your husband and was in some way close to him – a pocket watch, for example. In itself it is unimportant and can do nothing, it simply acts as a focus for my thoughts.'

She lifted her hands from the bag she was holding on her knee. 'Take this. I had some idea that you would want an item he was attached to and he used it whenever he went away – he had done so since he got it from his father, as a young man. It was still perfectly serviceable, just well-used, he always said, when I tried to persuade him that he needed a new one. He had it with him at the Tabor Club, it contained his night things and so forth, though when found it was empty.'

I took the bag and set it on my desk. It was a brown travelling bag, rather like a doctor's Gladstone bag, the leather a little cracked, the handles worn and repaired. I looked carefully inside but there was nothing.

'Might this be useful to you?'

'It will do perfectly.'

I asked her to return in two days time, at five o'clock. I might have asked her to come back the following day, as I planned to work on the case that night – I always find it best to make an immediate start, if I find that a case is 'warm'. One of the reasons I do not take on many is that they so often feel quite 'cold' to me.

But Sir Silas Webb's travelling bag was not cold. I had felt a heat around it the instant I touched it, and a charge, as if it gave off some mild static electricity. I do not employ any trickery and there would be no point in stagey effects as I always work alone, in the privacy of my study.

After supper, I placed the travelling bag on the table in front of me and settled back in my chair. The curtains were draw against the night and I had a single lamp switched on in the corner. I silenced the telephone. And then I simply sat still and focused on the bag, not only my gaze but my whole concentration, as if I were directing a beam of light at it. I sometimes wait like this for twenty or thirty minutes without anything happening at all. My energy and concentration are then depleted and I must go away, returning to focus on the object for another session the following day.

Sometimes, the moment I begin again I will feel an immediate connection, though I have no idea why a delay should have been necessary. If I feel nothing this second time, I do not try again – it would be pointless. Occasionally, I know at once that something is going to happen and this was the case when I sat down in front of the travelling bag. I felt a slight tingling in my fingers which quickly extended up my arms. At the same time, my vision, which is normally perfect, became a little cloudy, as if I were looking at the bag through a veil or a fine mist.

I waited quietly and soon this cleared, and at once I seemed to be looking, not directly at the bag itself, but at something in the space just before it. It came closer, it became clearer, and then the bag faded into the background. The room itself seemed to recede. It is like watching an old-fashioned magic lantern show, yet it is both more lucid than that and more lifelike. It seems to surround me and then I know that I am watching not a film or any other sort of performance. I am watching real life. The past is being replayed but I am not part of it, I remain firmly in my own world and place and time.

I was looking into a bedroom in some small hotel – there were no ornaments or any of the other para-phernalia of a lived-in home. It was very neat and tidy and the furniture was simple – a mahogany wardrobe, a table and upright chair, a bed and bedside cabinet. There was a washbasin with mirror above in the far corner, a shelf containing a few of the sort

38

of old books which are often placed in such a room but rarely read – a bible, a London companion, and two or three leather-bound novels by Dickens and Sir Walter Scott. A man's jacket was hanging up and a pair of shoes was beside the door, waiting to be put out for polishing. The leather travelling bag, the same bag on which my eyes had first focused, was on the bed.

As I watched, the door opened, and a man wearing evening clothes came in. I recognised him, from occasional newspaper photographs, as Sir Silas Webb. He was not tall but he had a pompous way of carrying himself which made him appear so. His face was smooth, and his nose and mouth had a faintly sneering set. His complexion was flushed, as if he had enjoyed several glasses of good port. I watched as he went to the mirror, undid his black tie and took the studs out of his collar. He then went to the travelling bag and put it down on the table. It was at this exact point that there crept over me a sense of claustrophobia, and an increasing fear, which made me sit back in my chair. My heart was beating too fast and sweat beads were forming on my forehead and across the back of my neck, and all of this increased as I watched the man open the travelling bag by the top clasp.

As the two sides spread wide, I caught my breath in horror. Moths had begun to emerge from the bag's interior, at first one or two small, pale moths and then flights of them, becoming larger and darker, with ugly furred heads and queerly patterned wings, streaked and marked as if with small faces and skulls and tiny glaring eyes. They poured out and as they did so, flew around Silas Webb's head, pattered against his hands and face. Some of them made for the lamp, while others seemed to flutter about like blind things, as they emerged, rising to the ceiling and touching it before falling down again in the dark corners of the room, onto the top of the wardrobe, but always returning, to fly about the head of the stricken man. He beat his arms madly to try to brush them away, and all the time his face was working with terror, and ghastly pale. I heard him moan, then cry out for help, then scream, I saw him spin round and back, shouting hoarsely now, as the great moths and their soft, powdery bodies and endlessly fluttering, batting wings, seemed to be attacking his very person.

My own throat was dry and the sweat was running down my face. The scene appeared to last for several hours and yet it was over in moments. Webb put his hand up to his breast, his face contorted with pain, and then crashed to the floor. The moths dispersed harmlessly into the folds of the curtains, and now there appeared to be far fewer of them, and they were smaller in size than they had looked when they were pouring out of the travelling bag. Several camouflaged themselves against the wallpaper but then seemed to dissolve into it, until they were all gone and the room was deathly silent and still.

I came to myself as the picture before me shrivelled to a single dot, before disappearing. I do not fall into any sort of 'trance' on these occasions, I am fully conscious and awake, but I have been focusing intently on one thing, and when it is no longer there, I have a moment's disorientation.

What I had just seen was horrible. A man had died of shock – heart failure indeed – because of what was surely some prank, such as schoolboys might play. But schoolboys mean no harm and if such harm as this ever came about as a result of their tricks, they would be appalled.

My concern was that although I now knew what had happened to Sir Silas Webb, I had no idea why or who could have played such a vile game. I also knew that I would almost certainly never find out.

I now had the choice of telling Lady Webb the truth, thereby distressing her beyond measure, to little purpose, or of taking my story to the police. I had friends in the force to whom I could go privately and who knew of my work, but they would be obliged to ask me for evidence and I had none. I could also undertake a wearisome and probably fruitless private investigation.

I decided quickly that I would do none of these things. I would tell Lady Webb that I had discovered enough to be sure that her husband had indeed died of heart failure – 'natural causes'. It was the plain truth. For my own interest and satisfaction, I intended to do just one more thing, though I was doubtful that it would yield any result.

I wondered, when I was going over the events in my mind late into that night, what had happened to the moths. Surely a great many would have been found by the cleaners. But they would probably have brushed and swept the room even more vigorously than usual, in the light of the sudden death that had occurred there. Moths do not live very long and their fragile bodies would have crumbled into dust.

I half-thought of asking to see into the room that Webb had died in. but what reason could I have given? I had certainly no wish to seem like a ghoul.

Six

I had signalled for more brandy for us both. We needed it. I let the fiery liquid slip down my throat before saying, in as relaxed a manner as I could, 'And there you have it, Tom. Something and nothing, perhaps. But you asked for my most unusual and intriguing story and, perhaps because we are within the four walls of the club again, that was the one which came to mind immediately.'

'Horrible,' Tom said with a shudder, and drinking deeply. 'What a dastardly, wicked trick to play. I would hope the man has not slept easily in his bed since he learned of its terrible outcome. What did you say to Lady Webb, as a matter of interest?'

'Exactly as I had decided.'

'And she accepted it?'

'She appeared to do so. I have heard nothing from her since.'

'And what of the travelling bag?'

'She took it away. I might have suggested that she destroy it, except that she had stressed how devoted her husband had been to it. She clasped it to her and I daresay it has become a "sacred relic" – women tend towards the keeping of these memento mori, you know.'

We left the club to go our separate ways home. Tom thanked me for entertaining him with 'a most disturbing tale. I wonder how well I shall sleep tonight?'

'You asked for it, my dear fellow, you asked for it.'

I saw him into a cab but then set off to walk the mile or so to my own house. It was a crisp, starry night and a full moon sailed over the dome of St Paul's, a thin, sparkling trace of rime around it. The streets were quiet and my mind turned once again to my story.

From what I had heard since, Sir Silas had not been especially likeable but he deserved no less than any other man and I sent up a heartfelt prayer for the peace and rest of his soul. There was nothing more that I could do.

Seven

The Conclusion: Walter Craig's Story

It is many years since the death of Silas Webb, which gave me no joy or satisfaction, however much I had come to despise the man for having achieved worldly honours and acclaim via the work of another. He had stolen, cheated, lied and dissembled and I had become more and more embittered and resentful. And, alongside those feelings, dark and hot as boiling tar, the desire for personal revenge had swollen, like a monstrous abscess within me, until I could bear it no longer and felt that I must lance it by some violent action.

I had meant to terrify the man, to give him a hellish hour, to leave him an ashen-faced, stuttering wreck, with flayed nerves and a terror of what might be to come. But as God is my witness, I had never meant to harm let alone to kill him. It had never occurred to me that he might drop down dead from overwhelming fear. When I heard that he had died suddenly of heart failure, I was shaken out of myself, appalled, and quite sure of my own guilt, certain that it was my actions that had made his heart stop. I could say nothing to anyone. The Coroner's verdict had been given and the obsequies performed. Only I knew. Only I knew what Webb had done to me. I would have to carry that secret with me, along with my own guilt, until the end of my days.

I might have prayed that, somehow, I would get my just deserts. I did not, if only because I had no belief in any power to whom I might appeal. My conviction was that I would die, as Webb had died, of a sudden clutching at the heart – but that was a mere superstition. I had no idea how my death would come. And so I carried on my dull and insignificant life, walking in shadow.

I retired from my academic post. I had long since lost my appetite and flair for scientific research but I managed to obtain a commission to write a student textbook. This did well and I embarked upon others. The work was not arduous, only painstaking, and I discovered that I had a natural ability to explain difficult concepts in clear and simple terms, something which gave me a measure of pride, after years of lacking any. I never forgot Silas Webb or what he and I, in our turn, had done to one another, but his name was certainly no longer at the front of my mind.

One evening, I came in late from the library, where I had been working on an index. It was October and my rooms were both chilly and dark, so I hastened to switch on the lamps, put a match to the fire and draw the curtains. As I touched the drape, something fluttered lightly against the back of my hand, the touch so gentle that I barely felt it, and a moth flew out and made straight for a lamp. It was bone-coloured and not large, with faint rusty etchings on its wing tips.

I had never been troubled by fear of moths, or of any other insects. If I was I would never have been able to do what I did to Silas Webb's travelling bag. I was a man without phobias of any kind. I had never minded small closed spaces, heights, or even my own childhood bedroom, when a small fire glowing in the grate sent monstrous shadows up the walls. I had thought of them as friendly.

The quick flight of the moth gave me a start but then, and for the first time, I felt a slight revulsion. I did not care for the tiny proboscis which jutted from between the pulsating wings. I recoiled from the sound of its pattering on the parchment lamp shade, as the two somehow camouflaged one another.

I did not stay reading the evening paper by the lamp's light because I was unnerved by the proximity of the moth to my head. I made ready for bed but, as I folded the paper, I caught sight of the date. It set up some echo in my memory, though I could not place it, but I woke in the middle of the night to recall clearly that 24 October had been the date of Silas Webb's death – a death for which I had surely been responsible.

I reached out to switch on the bedside lamp. I would drink a glass of water before settling back to sleep. All was still. I shrugged off thoughts of the calendar and lay down, but as I did so, something tremulous and feathery settled on my face and rested there.

After that night, what I thought of as 'the persecution', continued. I was haunted and pursued by moths evening and night, and in time they became larger. I never knew when they would appear: silent, soft and purposeful, they always caught me by surprise. Days, sometimes a week or two, would go by, until I relaxed and convinced myself that there was nothing strange or menacing about any of it. Just as there are autumn seasons when wasps are rare and others when they are like a biblical plague, so it was with these moths. There was some explanation in nature, to do with ambient temperature, food supply – who knew?

Then, just as I was easy, one would shock me, flying suddenly out of a cupboard, or be at rest, splayed motionless on a curtain or playing dead on my coat sleeve. I battled with them, I sprayed them with poison, and, if I could, I stamped or beat them to death; and with all of this, I became more and more afraid. I ceased to visit the old section of the science library, after one had flown out of a book I opened. At night, I drew my curtains slowly and with a pole. I slept badly, the moths fluttering through my dreams and turning them to nightmares. I felt them settle on my arm or my face in the darkness, and in the end I slept buried beneath the bedclothes, trembling with fear.

Gradually, I became afraid of more and more creatures and of everything furry: birds, rodents, even cats. I could not work. My heart was always racing, my nerves frayed with the effort of remaining alert and afraid.

And so it has been. But now, as I write this, cowering at my desk in the half-dark, I see that it is past ten o'clock on a May evening and I have spent some time looking at the gardens and the freshly leafed and blossoming trees from my window – for I cannot go out. I have been struck by a peculiar paralysis, which clamps down upon me towards the end of every afternoon. It creeps over me like ice, freezing my body slowly. I cannot walk. If I take a chair, I am quickly locked where I sit. My arms become helpless, my head will not turn. I can see and hear and breathe but I cannot utter a sound.

I will be possessed and kept helpless until some point the next morning. I have tried running away from here but the moment I take a step towards the door, the paralysis overcomes me at once. Only if I remain in my rooms am I allowed some remission.

My landlady brings me food and I am able to spend a few hours of each day working at my desk.

And even if I were permitted to escape, where would I go? Where could I flee to, without being hunted down and attacked? I am safest here in my comfortable prison. I would even be quite happy, were it not for the gathering dusk, the waning of the light, the approach of night. Then I must endure the torments he endured, the emergence of the moths from every crack and crevice, from behind the curtains and between their folds, from beneath cushions and below chairs, from the pages of books and from the backs of pictures, from carpet and from rug, giving birth to more and more, from out of the very dust of the air. I am assailed by the rising, teeming, fluttering clouds of them, they alight on me, they catch in my hair and leave their powdery traces on my skin. They are silent and menacing and I am their victim and must endure them. They do not hurt me, they only terrify. Sometimes they smell faintly of dust and decay. They are agile, alert, with glittering pin-pricks of eyes, and yet also dead, desiccated. Sometimes, I fancy that I see the cloudy image of Silas Webb's face within the pattern of their massed wings and bodies, but that must surely be a fantasy conjured up by my feverish mind and the terror, which is out of all control.

The horror may last an hour or a night, two minutes or two hours. I have no sense of time. It is out of time. I pray to be like Webb, taken by sudden death.

But Silas Webb has his revenge. Mine was so quick, so soon over, but I am his plaything, until he lets me go, on a whim – tomorrow? In a year? In twenty years? Or is this for eternity? I do not know. I only know that the end will not come now, not tonight, not yet. The ice is moving up my body and already I cannot move my legs. Dusk is swallowing up the sky, the rooftops, the trees, the gardens, and very soon I shall become aware of soft wings and bodies, closing in upon me, seething silently among themselves.

BOY
TWENTY-ONE

CLOTEN HOUSE BLAZE

A seventeenth-century stately home has been left a shell after devastating fire yesterday. The blaze, believed to have been caused by an electrical fault, started in the basement and ripped quickly through the building, which was empty at the time, spreading through the roof voids.

Cloten Hall, which is owned by National Heritage, is closed during the winter months but was due to reopen at Easter. It was acquired for the charity in 1990, after having been in the Dyker-Venn family for nearly 430 years. The family shrank in size to one pair of elderly brothers, Albert and Montague Dyker-Venn, who lived in the house alone until both men died, within a month of one another, in 1990. They had become impoverished, and the house and grounds were in a state of decay and disrepair.

'It was in a time-warp,' a spokesperson said, 'and in some ways, it was a magical place, where nothing had been modernised, changed, removed or renovated for generations. The gardens were

overgrown – it was like somewhere out of a fairy tale.'

When National Heritage acquired the property they took the decision to restore both house and contents, but 'with the lightest possible hand'. Teams of conservation experts took six years to repair and renovate both the building and ninety-five per cent of its contents, bringing the past back to life and light, without damaging or destroying its most valuable attribute: the atmosphere.

'We tried to retain the sense of period, and bring out the sense of Cloten as having always been a family home, never any sort of museum and certainly not a rich man's palace. We had to be more ruthless with the gardens and grounds, which were hopelessly overgrown, with dangerous trees, hidden, overgrown ponds, and crumbling statuary and outbuildings. Quite a lot had to be sacrificed, but garden experts of the period advised on re-design and planting. With the aid of plans and later photographs, all found in the house, it was brought slowly back to life, as it might once have been – though gardens take much longer to develop and mature than buildings. Cloten Hall was unique. None of our properties resemble it at all. It is very sad indeed to see it gutted by fire like this.'

No decision has yet been taken about the future of the building.

There was a photograph on the front page of the newspaper and another inside. Smoke. Flames. Water from the cannons arching up into the night sky, and cascading into the heart of the inferno.

Then, Cloten Hall in the early morning light, an aerial picture looking down into the gutted shell of the interior, like a half-built doll's house, with walls and floors and half-burned staircases, no roof, cinders for furniture.

I was on the bus going home. I have quite a long journey to work, on two buses with a mile walk at either end. Sometimes I complain, but others have it so much worse and at least I don't have to travel on the tube. I would find that unbearable. Indeed, I do not think I could do my job at the present place if I had to travel on anything that went underground.

Normally, at this point in my journey, I would turn to the Mind Games page. I am a keen crossword solver, though my record is not one hundred per cent. If quotations or celebrities or classical mythology are involved, I do badly. But I am pleased to say that I have not yet failed to complete a Sudoku success-fully. I find it the most satisfying of challenges. The completed grid gives me almost physical pleasure.

Tonight, though, I was preoccupied with the photographs of Cloten Hall, and the account of its burning. I thought about it for the rest of my journey home, and when I arrived, I did nothing but think about it again, not even turning on the lights but simply sitting in my armchair, going over things from so many years ago, letting my unconscious send individual details and snippets of memory, like bubbles, to the surface.

I had no newspaper here but when I turned on my television for the news, there it was, Cloten Hall, charred black and still smoking a little. I turned down the sound. I did not want some reporter giving me the story of the fire, or worse, a potted history of the place. I did not want their mock-solemn face in front of me. What did they know of what it meant to me? How could they possibly care?

Cloten Hall.

I did not eat that night. I went to bed and knew that I would not sleep for hours. I lay on my back, with the light out and the amber street lamp washing over the wardrobe, the bed quilt, the wall behind the bed. My face and hands. It was something like the glow from a dying fire itself.

I asked myself a host of questions. But the only question that mattered was the one to which I knew I could never find the answer.

Had he been there? Was he consumed in the flames, along with the oak and elm, the elaborate mouldings, the magnificent vaulted Long Gallery, the hidden staircase? Or had he left long before, perhaps because he could find no one else, as he once found me?

I dozed, and in my dreams, I saw and heard the crackling of flames. I smelled the smoke and the acrid burning. I saw him, standing in the Long Gallery. And sitting on my own bed, and then lying on the floor beside it, white-faced and frail, tears running down his face.

I saw him and held out my hand to him, and in my dreams, he smiled and stepped out of the fire and reached for the hand, smiling at me. Smiling.

One

'Mrs Mills?'

The boy Toby Garrett had emerged silently from the shadows of Bell Corridor, thin as a blade and with anxious eyes.

'Odd boy,' the headmaster had said more than once.

'Unhappy boy.'

'What makes you think that?'

But she had not wanted to go into it, afraid of sounding vague and sentimental, which Royce disliked.

Unhappy boy. Yes.

'Hello, Toby.'

'Mrs Mills …', he scraped his toe backwards and forwards, tracing the curve of a floor tile, head down.

'Is something wrong?'

'I like it here.'

She waited.

'Can I stay?'

She wondered. As far as she knew there had been no talk of Toby's leaving *Hesterly*.

'Can I be a boarding boy? Please. I mean now, today.'

His face puckered.

'Toby, I have to go to take a class. Will you come and see me at the end of the afternoon, in the Quiet Room?'

'Can't you say yes now, please. I want to stay now.'

'No. Four o'clock, all right?'

She had to turn away from such desperation, such pleading.

He was already waiting for her at the door of the Quiet Room, moving from one foot to the other, his body tuned tight.

'Can I stay? Have you asked?'

'It isn't for me to say, Toby, or not just me. It has to come from your parents, it ...'

'They will say yes. They will ... please?'

'Why is it so urgent?'

And then the story, of vicious rows and rage at home, of screaming and fists beaten against walls and heavy things thrown, of storms of crying and his mother's bleeding face. The terrifying boom of his father's fury.

'I'd be safe here,' the boy had said.

'Listen to me, Toby, look at me and please tell me the truth. Does your father – does anyone – hit you?'

He shook his head. 'They don't see me,' he said.

Divorce was nothing out of the ordinary, here as everywhere else, but probably domestic violence was uncommon among the parents – infidelity, boredom, alcohol, even, but not mothers being beaten in front of their thirteen-year-old sons.

'They will say yes.'

Yes.

A place was found within the week; his things were brought. No one seemed interested in when the boy would be returning home.

What would happen at Christmas?

'He will go to my brother,' the father had said. 'Cousins his age. Or an aunt.'

'Can't I stay here at Christmas?' The boy had been folding his pyjamas carefully, the trousers exactly edge to edge, then lining the edge exactly with that of the pillow.

*

Campion. Houseparents Graham and Mel Taylor. Easy-going. Comfortable. No long dormitories now, bedrooms with four or six boys. Their own duvet covers. Two small posters each. Lockers. Photographs. Parents. Siblings. Dogs. Teddy bears. Lego models.

Toby Garrett had no photographs.

'Would you like me to find you a poster, Toby? Until you can have your own sent from home maybe?'

'No, thank you.'

But he had a book of maps and a notebook in which he drew his own, invented countries. He had a second notebook, in which he made lists. Lists of anything. He knew two of the others in the room. They were casually welcoming. The bed next to his was empty.

He slept deeply and silently. Luke Beecham mumbled, David O'Hare turned over and back, over and back. Toby lay still as a log. Safe. It was quite new to him, this feeling of safety, and he trusted it.

'Who used to be in the other bed?'

'Jack Murdoch. He left. They moved to somewhere like Africa.'

'Someone else will come though,' O'Hare said. 'The school needs the money.'

The 'someone' came three days later. His name was Andreas.

'Where do you come from?'

'I don't know.'

The other two hooted. 'He doesn't know where he came from?', and pushed each other about, laughing false laughter.

'Leave him alone. He just forgot.'

David O'Hare widened his eyes. Luke rolled his.

'Toby can tell you where you came from. He's got maps. He loves maps. He adores maps. Maps are his babies.'

They fell on the floor and rolled about, knees up, shrieking.

Toby turned and looked at the new boy in the next bed.

'It doesn't matter if you don't know.'

Andreas fidgeted with his bedcover, his fingers plucking at the seam.

'Were they kind where you came from?'

'Quite kind.'

'How long were you there?'

'I don't know. It felt like a long time. Quite a while?'

His face went strangely blank, as if he had taken

his real self off somewhere, his mind and his soul, Toby thought, and just left the body.

After that first night, they were inseparable, somehow even when they were in different classes, playing different games. They separated themselves politely from the rest, did not share time with any of them, only with each other. They were silent together when they worked, chairs next to one another, and they ate in the dining room in the same way. If Toby did not like the meat he passed his to Andreas. Andreas did not drink milk or eat any pudding made with milk. He passed his dish and Toby ate it, as well as his own. They walked outside together, sat against the library wall in the sun and read or pulled up grass stalks and chewed them. Andreas swam like a fish. Toby was afraid of water. Within a month, he had conquered his fear and followed the patient Andreas, doing as he did, learning to float, copying the strokes. Then Andreas arrowed out across the pool, swift and graceful, turned underwater, swam back ahead of everyone, and Toby watched, unsmiling but with his face showing his admiration, his pride, without shame.

At night, they talked quietly, beds pushed closer together so that the other two were not disturbed. Could not overhear.

Their stories were very different, their feelings identical.

Toby lay in bed one night, on his side so that he faced Andreas. Moonlight washed over his face. His hair was thick, wavy and black; his skin was dark olive. His arm was outstretched in the direction of Toby's bed.

He had been sitting with his mother when she had started to breathe in a strange way and her eyes had looked at him in panic, then they had clouded and he had thought she was not seeing him any more. He had touched her arm and then her face, and spoken to her, told her to listen to him. He had begun to shake her gently.

The maid had come in, looked at the woman in the bed, and started to pull Andreas away from her, gripping his arm so hard that her fingers left marks, and at the same time she had been calling out to his uncle, to anyone in the house.

It had been his uncle who came, taking hold of Andreas, lifting him up and carrying him out of the room. As he was carried away, he thought he saw a bloom of blood spreading across the front of his mother's nightdress, staining the white cloth red.

'I kicked,' he said to Toby, 'I kicked him hard. I tried to push my fingers into his eyes.'

'What happened to your mother?'

'She was dead. They didn't let me see her again. They wouldn't let me go back and kiss her.'

'What about your father?'

'He died in the war. They said my mother never got over it.'

'What war?'

But Andreas seemed confused, unsure. Toby was silent, holding deep inside himself a confused ball of bewilderment and pain he did not know how to express. His own mother might die. His father might kill his own mother. He would be alone with his father. Andreas had been sent away but he might be sent back home, and made to stay there.

'Say a word,' Andreas said. 'Only not "sorry".'

But there was no other word that could be said.

He did not speak about himself, simply because Andreas did not ask him. They shared time, space, silence, and odd games with complicated rules they created, and which had fluid structures, ebbing and flowing.

Toby drew maps and labelled them intricately, and from the maps emerged imaginary countries, kingdoms, islands, cities. Tribes. Communities. Languages.

They read the same books, each beginning one and exchanging when they had finished.

They were quite friendly to other boys but kept a small space between themselves and anyone else, and the other boys stopped noticing and got on with their own lives, sometimes looking, whispering, mostly ignoring, shrugging their shoulders.

But the adults noticed and kept a wary eye, and spoke about it among themselves, and proposed solutions.

'Solutions to what? It's a friendship. Two lonely and vulnerable boys.'

'Such an intense one, and they shut everyone else out. It's unhealthy.'

'They're thirteen years old, for God's sake!'

'I might suggest moving them into different rooms in *Campion*.'

'Which would be cruel and, in my view, counter-productive.'

'Move sets?'

'Don't do anything at all. Let it work itself out.'

There seemed to be no solution and so the matter was shelved and the boys continued as they were, always together, often silent. They knew, without being able to articulate what they knew, that they had found a solace and a healing and did not question it or look beyond the day, although once, when the summer holidays were mentioned, Andreas simply said, 'You'll come with me.'

Toby did not doubt it.

Two weeks before the end of term, Andreas disappeared. He was not in his place next to Toby at lunch. Toby was silent, eyes watching the door, waiting.

The others kept a little apart from him, puzzled, even afraid. No one knew anything.

At eight, they went up to bed. The other two had undressed quickly, turned away, David O'Hare with his head in a book, Luke deep under the duvet.

Andreas's bed was empty and unmade. It had been pushed into the corner, beneath the window.

'Goodnight boys, sleep well.'

Lights out.

He wanted to ask but feared the answer. He lay on his back, eyes open, looking at the line of soft light from the corridor, below the door, and the empty space next to him was so deep he might drown in it.

'Toby?'

He waited.

'Are you OK?'

'Yes, thank you.'

'I could come and sit on your bed if you wanted. If you can't go to sleep.'

'It's OK, thank you.'

He heard David shift his bedclothes about, then settle down. After that, there was only the light and the space next to him and his own wakefulness.

The term ended.

Toby waited in the entrance hall watching cars arrive, parents emerge, cars load up, people waving, and waving, watched the crowd of boys thin out, shrink to a small pool in the middle of the hall.

He prayed not to be the last and, by two boys, he wasn't. A blue car with a man he thought he recognised turned in front of the steps.

'Toby Garrett? Oh, there you are. Your uncle couldn't come, he's tied up in meetings, so I'm here. You remember me don't you?'

There was a hurried conference with two teachers, and the man disappeared and the last other boy left. It was hot.

'Sorry, had to see your head man, make sure I was all right ... you know. You remember me now?'

'I think so.'

'Martin Preece ... work with your uncle. Live across the other side?'

Toby thought he must know the man, everyone had agreed that he did and that it was all right.

His trunk and bags were loaded into the blue car. Only Mrs Mills stood watching them go, waving, not smiling.

A river ran through the garden of his uncle's house. Years after, he remembered lying on the grassy bank beside it, trailing his hands under the water, which turned them pale as peeled green sticks, the movement making them wave, frond-like, gently to and fro. He liked to feel the coolness slipping over them.

There was no one else at the house that summer. He decided not to mind. He went with his uncle's wife into the market town ten miles away and helped carry her shopping, stood beside her when she talked to people, and drank a milk shake in the café while she had coffee. She was kind to him but said very little – he decided it was because she had no children and so did not know how to talk to them. He rarely saw his uncle. He went to London very early, came back late. Once or twice he took Toby out in his car at the weekends, or to swim or to fish, but he hated the thought of the barb hooking itself into the roof of the fish's mouth, of the way it cheated and deceived the creature, which was only looking for food.

It was hot. He remembered it years afterwards as the time when his skin always felt warm, unless he was dabbling in the river.

He also remembered clearly the first time he saw the other boy. He had been looking down at the frond of bright green weed, like hair waving under the water, feeling the sun on the back of his head. He saw his own reflection, waving slightly too, and then he saw the other one, just behind him. The face was thoughtful, and as if he were far away, and his arms were spread out by his sides. He floated. Toby turned slowly and looked behind him, then above, then at the opposite side of the river. But there was no one. No other boy.

He went down two or three times every day, even when there was rain, and waited, and looked at himself in the clear water as it slid by. Waited. Once, there was a shadow. He thought there was a shadow. Once, he was sure that the other boy's face and outstretched arms were there, actually there, and yet not visible.

That was all.

It was not a bad summer. The days passed. He made lists of fish, and rivers. He read a lot of the books in his uncle's den, books he had had as a boy. *The*

Wonder Book of the RAF. A Boy's Army Adventure. Seb Seamer, Secret Spy. The Wonder Book of Transport. They had more drawings than coloured pictures, and everything was old-fashioned, in a comforting way.

There was only one thing wrong, one thing which soured the summer, and that was the absence of Andreas. He missed him every day. He turned to tell him something, show him something, laugh with him, shove him so that Andreas would shove back and they could have a scramble-fight, walk alongside him, chewing grass blades, hear him breathing close by when he woke in the night. He asked his uncle if Andreas would ever come back but then realised that he had never heard of Andreas.

Something had shrivelled inside him. The space Andreas had occupied was hollow and silent.

Two

'Is that everybody? I should have twelve boys from *Campion*, and eight from *Cranmer*. I'll count heads as you get onto the coach. Has everyone been to the loo? Because you won't be able to go for a couple of hours, we're not stopping at every service station. Right, first pair, up the steps please. One … two … three … careful … seven … Lucas Johnson, are you chewing something?'

Toby waited towards the back. It was the last week in September and as sunny and warm as July. He pictured the stream. His hands trailing in the water.

Where was Andreas now?

'Come on Toby Garrett, miles away as usual.'

But he looked better for the summer holidays, his skin brown, his face less taut with anxiety. His eyes were always far away. She still worried about the boy.

'Where is it?'

'Can't remember.'

'Cloten Hall.'

'House.'

'Well, anyway.'

'What is it?'

'Haven't a clue but it's bound to be boring.'

Toby sat next to a boy from *Cranmer* who had only four fingers on his left hand.

'I've been to this place before.'

'Is it like a castle?'

'No.'

'Did you go with Mrs Mills?'

'No.'

'Now, listen up please. I hope you didn't think you were going to spend the journey chatting about England's chances against the West Indies and whether the shop will sell sweets.' Mrs Mills wobbled as the coach veered left.

'Can everybody hear me?'

'You should have one of those microphone things like they do on the tourist buses, Mrs Mills.'

'I should but the school doesn't run to it so pin back your ears instead. Right ... Cloten Hall. Does anybody know when it was built? Not the day or the month or even the year, the century will do. No? Why am I not surprised? Cloten Hall ... and by the way, you will be doing a full project on it, including an essay, divided into several parts, so don't go off into a daydream, you need to remember. Right ... In 1760 or thereabouts ...'

Toby looked out of the coach window. Fields. Houses. Motorway. Fields. Lanes. Houses. Blue sky. Sun suddenly flashing into his eyes.

Where was Andreas? Had he gone home to his father? Was he in his own country? Whatever country that was, and Toby had never been quite sure. Why had he come and gone so quickly? Did he remember *Hesterly*? Mrs Mills's voice in his ears.

Jacobean. Which James was that? Tapestry. The Dyker-Venn family. Royal marriage. The Battle of ... House crumbling. Roof fell in. Birds nested. Bats. Dust. Walls breaking down. Thickets. Brambles. Green ponds. A well. The Long Gallery. The same family had owned it for ... for ...

'Over three hundred years ... but by then ...'

Two old men. One old servant. One room. Maybe two. Roof leaking. Damp. Mould even. No electricity. Front door bolted with iron bolts for decades. Horses and servants and dogs and ... nobody. No cars. No money. Iron ranges. Iron pans. Iron beds.

The king had slept there. Which king? Why? When?

James.

Jacobean.

Tapestries.

Paintings with mould and cracks and soot congealed. Van Dyke. Horses. Rusting bridles. Rust. Deathwatch beetle. And darkness.

Dark everywhere. Creepers grew up the windows. Even in summer, darkness. Candles. Torches on window ledges, with dead flies and beetles and tarnished silver dishes.

The old men died there.

Preserved. Time warp, like a fairy story. Thickets and thorns grew round. Light coming through the windows, filtered through leaves and branches, green, as if it were under sea.

In spite of themselves, they listened as she wove the magic spell. Which made their first sight of the house a disappointment.

'You said there was a tent of cobwebs.'

'Where is all the dust?'

Cloten Hall, rescued just as it was about to crumble and fall, restored, repainted, re-gilded, refurbished. Polished. Clean.

The creeper pulled off the front, the gardens shaven and re-laid.

A tall house, with pointed gables. Stone mullions. It stood at the end of a long drive and looked down on everyone who walked towards it, humbling them. They got into the entrance hall first.

'You will see how the lower half of the walls are covered in wood panelling. Why do you think that is?'

Above the panelling, dark pictures, men in women's clothes, women like pantomime dames, skirts like barrels. Small dogs. Horses. Long, long, dark oak tables. High-backed dark oak chairs. Settles. Long, long dark red carpets running through the hall, the first room, the second room.

'The house was built by a very rich man around the year 1630. Can anyone tell me who was on the throne of this country in 1630?'

Beyond the hall a corridor stretched away. At the end, a tall window. Beneath the window, an oak bench.

A boy was sitting on the bench. Glancing away from the teacher and the fireplace and the rest of the group for a moment only, Toby saw him. He was very still. He had dark hair, worn long with thick curls. Some sort of tunic.

'Andreas?'

'Toby Garrett, are you with the rest of us in 1630 or in some other era?'

He mumbled sorry. Turned his head back to the portrait they were looking at. The man who built Cloten Hall. He wore a strange black hat, had cruel, arching eyebrows. Haughty.

When he looked down the corridor again, the boy had gone.

They trailed round. Worksheets were handed out. Toby bent his head over an ancient chest with iron bands. The others were here and there, scribbling, reading questions, asking this and that of Mrs Mills, sketching rough plans.

He edged his way towards the group at the back of the room and concealed himself between two of the boys. Nobody noticed. Mrs Mills turned her back and was pointing something out on the far wall.

He slipped away like a shadow.

There was a staircase, shallow stone steps, curving round. He made no sound.

The house seemed to be empty apart from them.

An open door and then he felt as if he were Jonah inside the whale, the belly of the long gallery. An oak trunk set every few yards against each wall.

An oak bench between. The roof was the whale's ribcage, panelled and carved, and painted white. It ran towards the window at the far end. A high window. The sunlight was like golden sword blades falling onto the floor.

He was there, looking, waiting.

'Andreas?'

He said nothing. Toby walked very softly, very slowly down the long empty room.

He was Andreas. And yet he was changed. His skin was paler. His hair longer. But he sat in the same calm, still way, waiting. Looking.

'Is this where you came from? Is this where you've been? Is this where you live?'

The other boy smiled.

Toby went closer and made to sit down but at once the boy was up and moving swiftly away, down the gallery.

'Don't go. Please. I've wanted to see you ever since … Andreas?'

The boy stopped.

'Why won't you talk to me?'

The boy turned. They were close enough now.

It might not be Andreas after all. The boy did not speak, did not move, did not smile, as Andreas had. And yet it was Andreas. He knew. He was sure.

'Toby Garrett?'

Footstep after footstep, coming up the stone stairs.

'What do you think you're doing? You know perfectly well that you do *not* wander off on your own. Now come here, back to the group, and if you do that once more ... Now, boys, stand here. Look down. This is one of the finest examples of a Jacobean barrelled ceiling in the country. Isn't it beautiful? Isn't it amazing? Look at the way each panel has been plastered and the plaster has been decorated ...'

He looked, and as he did so, the boy seemed to dissolve slowly, as if he were made of sherbet, touching the tongue. They went outside, released like birds from a cage, racing about. The dust in the air of the long gallery seethed in the wake of their leaving.

Toby went last. Looked back. Lances of sunlight. Plaster roof moulded like wedding cake.

No boy.

No Andreas.

'Come back. Please. Come back.' His whisper ran down the room.

No.

'Toby Garrett, down here. Now!'

'When are we going into the dungeons, Mrs Mills?'

81

'There aren't any dungeons, sorry, Adam.'

'Why not?'

'This isn't a castle.'

'Will we see the ghost?'

'There aren't any ...'

'There are, there are, it says here in the booklet, Mrs Mills ... it says ...'

'Of course it does. They want people to pay to come and see them. It's called a sales trick, Joshua. Five more minutes running about then you go back to the coach and get your packed lunches. Toby? Are you all right?'

'Yes, thank you.'

'Well, get up and run about then ... we're going into the kitchens and sculleries next. Have you got your worksheet?'

He sat on a grassy bank and opened his lunch pack. Sam Hilder stood over him.

'You're weird, Garrett.'

He could have said that he knew.

'Sorry.'

'What for?'

He opened his egg and tomato sandwich and bit into it hard. It was Sam's finger. The tomato was his blood.

'What's wrong with you?'

'Nothing.'

'You're weird.'

Toby sighed and looked round Hilder, to the back of the house that reared up behind him. At one of the top windows he saw a face. A head and shoulders. Pale. Black hair.

It dissolved.

Perhaps he had not seen it.

'You OK, Tobes?'

David O'Hare was all right. He'd been friendly. Kind. To him. To Andreas.

'He's weird.'

'Piss off Hilder. You stink.'

O'Hare sat beside him on the grass and crunched into his apple. The sun was warm on their faces.

'There is a ghost,' David said. 'A woman. She died of a broken heart. Her husband got killed in the civil war. She glides up the staircase.'

'I didn't see her.'

'Nor did I. Cable's pretending he did. He said she had blood on the front of her dress where her heart was. Do you believe in them? Ghosts?'

Toby crammed sandwich into his mouth quickly.

Yes. No.

Yes.

'I'm not sure,' David O'Hare said, getting up. 'See you.'

'See you.'

Where David had flattened the grass down, Andreas sat now. He had no lunch pack. He looked at Toby.

'Where did you go? Why did you? I wish you hadn't have gone.'

But the grass sprang back and Andreas was no longer there.

The coach came round to the front at two-thirty.

'Good,' David O'Hare said. 'That was mega boring.'

'The stables were OK.'

'There weren't any horses in them.'

Toby was with Harry Fletcher, five pairs down the queue.

'Right, single file from here please. You know the drill … stop as you are about to get onto the coach and wait till I've counted you before you do.'

Shuffle forwards.

'One … off you go … two … three … Get a move on, Edward … four …'

Toby looked back at the house. Every window that he could see. One, two, three, four … but there was no one.

Five …

Was the boy Andreas? He was like him. Very like him. But was it *him*?

'Seventeen … eighteen … nineteen … twenty … twenty-one … Stop. Isaac Wemyss. Go back. Right. Who was in front of you?'

'Ben.'

'Yes. Ben, come back here please. Get off again … just do it, Ben. Thank you. Right, Ben. Twenty. Isaac. Twenty-one.'

'Are you all right, Mrs Mills?'

'I am perfectly all right, thank you … but we left with twenty boys and we seem to be returning with twenty-one. Which is not possible.'

'Mrs Mills?'

'I'm sorry, Mr Gant, but they're all going to have to get off again. There can't possibly be an extra boy.'

'Better than one less.'

'I'm not so sure. Everybody, please listen. You are to get off the coach in the same order in which you got on just now … and line up here, as you were. Because I miscounted, George … but better be safe. Right, starting at the back please.'

*

Five minutes.

Ten.

'Fifteen … sixteen … seventeen … wait, Arthur, wait … right, eighteen, on you get then … nineteen. Twenty. Twenty-one.' Mrs Mills raised a white face.

In the end, there was nothing for it but for everyone to say that Mrs Mills had had a long, tiring day, perhaps wasn't feeling herself, and the bus left, with the teacher seated at the front, with a queer, dazed expression. But Toby had known at once. He had not seen Boy Twenty-One, but he had known all the same. He was on the back seat and Andreas was next to him. He did not have to see him. They talked.

They did not have to talk aloud. Their minds became their voices, their thoughts words.

He was still there when they got back to the school, but then, he was not there. There was a space where he had been at Toby's side. Perhaps that was how it would be again.

But when he woke in the night, he knew that the bed in which Andreas had slept next to him had been put back, and that the boy was in it sleeping. He did not need to reach out, to make sure by touching him. He was just there.

After that, he was always there, in classes, in the

dining room, on the playing fields, at prep. It felt safe again.

'Toby Garrett is a different boy.'

'He's working harder.'

'You find that? I think he's in a trance half the time.'

'At least it's a happier trance.'

'He's had a growth spurt.'

'Parents could do to take a bit more interest.'

It did not matter. He forgot his parents for days at a time. He forgot he had any parents. He was happy. The days passed. The weeks.

It ceased to feel strange that no one else saw the twenty-first boy. It was safer. No one else could take him away.

And then, he went. Like before, but not like that. He was simply there beside him as they walked down New Corridor, and then he was not there.

As he crossed the hall, boys were going out of the front door. He saw Angus, Will Baines, Joseph Needham, Kit Baker, Archie, from the parallel form.

'Don't,' Toby said to him, 'you're wrong, you mustn't go with them. You should stay here. Stay here.'

But he was already climbing onto the coach.

No need to ask where it was taking them.

Toby stood alone in the hall after the coach had driven off and his own class were on their way to the science block. He smelled the diesel that hung on the air, mingling with the smell of wallflowers.

Then he sat on the cold tiles and folded himself up, hunched his back, put his head down. He did not cry. He made no sound at all.

People walked round him.

People stopped.

Someone called his name.

Mrs Mills came after a few minutes, knelt down and talked to him, though he did not speak. He could not. In the end, she helped him up and took him away.

Three

I remember very little about that time. I am told that I did not speak for almost a year. I know I went to a clinic and that various people talked to me and tried to help. I know that I was taken away from *Hesterly* at the end of that term and was sent to a special school in Wales. I don't remember very much about what it was like there but I remember purple and grey mountains in the distance and a lake that seemed to stretch forever. I remember that it seemed easiest not to talk. There was nothing to say and I did not have any answers to their questions.

My parents were no longer together and I spent most time with my mother, whose eyes always seemed blank, and who lived as if she were muffled in blankets. I spent a lot of time alone, which I did not mind. I think I was just waiting.

But neither of them came back.

I never went to my uncle's place again. I was told that he had died and the house was sold.

I suppose the years passed and I grew up.

It is a long time ago. I live alone. I am better that way. My quiet job makes me feel safe, though I find the travelling difficult.

I draw maps. I invent countries and their histories, as I did with Andreas.

I had not thought about any of it for a long time, because I have found it better not to delve into the past. It upsets me.

And then I read in the newspaper about Cloten Hall.

I cannot sleep. I want to know what happened to him, where he was when the fire broke out, if he was saved, if he … if …

I want more than anything to go there and see for myself. I might be able to find him. I might rescue him. He might follow me, as he did onto the coach. The Extra Boy. Boy Twenty-One.

ALICE BAKER

Promises had been made for years that we would not have to put up with our cramped, dingy old offices for much longer but would be moving to new ones 'any day'. These would be spacious, light, quiet, and airy. We were even shown plans and given a presentation, with photographs, of the sort of building that would house us.

Nothing ever happened. Some people got tired of spending their working days in inadequately lit rooms, with their desks pressed too close to a wall or to that of another person, and they left. But others soon took their places, glad of the jobs, and having been spun stories about how they would only be working in this old building for a short time.

There were twelve of us when the new girl arrived. We had long made a pact that we would never reveal what we were sure was the true situation about the offices. It would be unfair to prick someone's happy balloon at the start, and besides, what did we actually *know*? So we smiled and nodded and kept our mouths shut. Otherwise, we were an amiable, easy-going bunch, good about contributing to the pool that provided cake on Friday afternoons and topping it up generously for birthdays. We chatted but not too much, and we never gossiped about one another, though we certainly told the tale about the bosses, and those who worked in the adjacent and upstairs rooms. We always took it in turns to help a new arrival, show them where everything was, teach them the vagaries of the photocopier, and demonstrate the trick of how to turn on the hot tap in the loo.

This season's new girl was called Alice Baker and she had already arrived when we got into work at nine o'clock. She was alone in the office, standing looking out of the window. When the first three of us piled in through the door, she turned and did not so much look at us as look us over, without any embarrassment. She seemed quite self-possessed – even oddly at home, as though she was perfectly familiar with the room and everything in it – including us.

It was April and the heating had been turned off but the office could still be chilly. Alice Baker wore a neat blue cotton frock, patterned with sprigs of small white flowers. She had neat hair, pulled off her face and coiled at the back. Neat Mary Jane shoes. I noticed straight away how small her feet were. Small feet and small hands.

'Good morning. I'm starting today.'

Her voice was pleasant, quiet but not whispery, and she had no accent of any sort.

After that, it was introductions, the section manager coming in and briefing her about this and that, which he would already have done when she was hired – but Malcolm liked to show that he was in charge. When he had gone, we told her what we thought she needed to know, said she should ask any of us if she had a problem – and settled down at our desks.

She had been given one at the back, beside the door – not a good place, because there was always a draught as people came and went, and when anyone walked down the corridor the desk shook. But it was the traditional place for a newcomer. If they were lucky, someone would leave and they could move, the place by the door being taken by the next newcomer. None of them dared to complain.

Our lunch hour was from half past twelve and most of us brought in sandwiches and we ate together, turning our chairs round to form a group. Sometimes, one or two people went out, to the Greek Cypriot café in the next street, where they served good soup and a dish of the day, which was almost always moussaka, but the queue was long from noon, and you could waste your break time standing in it.

Alice Baker settled down to work and hardly lifted her head at all that first morning. It was as if she had known everything for months, and had no queries. But three times, she got up and tried to wedge the door so that it stayed properly closed after someone had come through it. The third time, she looked over at Wendy.

'This is really annoying. Can no one do anything?'

The room went silent for a moment.

'Not really,' said Wendy, a girl who had never been disliked by anyone. 'It's the door. Everybody's tried – I'm afraid this ancient building is the real problem.'

'And two keys are sticking on my machine.'

'Here, let me …'

Dilys was another helpful one – actually, now I think of it, everybody in the room was like that. We just got on with one another and got on with the work.

I happened to glance as Dilys bent over Alice Baker's keyboard and as she did so, I saw a strange expression cross her face. It was not dislike but a sort of distaste. But then she went back to fiddling with the keyboard, and by the time she had finished her expression was normal and pleasant again.

'That's another thing,' she said, walking back

to her own desk, 'We're always being told we'll be given brand new machines when we move into these amazing new offices. Anyway, that should be OK for now.'

Alice Baker did not say thank you, merely nodded, and I thought her expression was strange, too, mostly because it was not an expression at all. She looked simply blank.

The old-fashioned building had one good feature, a leftover from better days, and that was the tea trolley, which came round every morning at eleven o'clock and every afternoon at three-thirty, laden with cakes, buns and biscuits, as well as drinks. On Alice Baker's first day, when the bell rang in the corridor, she jumped and asked in quite a panicky voice if that was the fire alarm. She was even standing up, as if she was ready to run. Christine explained, as we all started looking for handbags and purses.

'And you have to be smart because there's a queue and all the best cakes will have gone.'

At the end of the afternoon, some people would be straight out of the door, others would linger, chatting and gathering their things before leaving in twos and threes. There was a lift, a creaking lumbering thing whose ropes you could watch as they slid up and down like snakes, and whose light was usually out, so that you went down in pitch darkness, praying it didn't stop between landings, or plunge to the bottom of the shaft. Not a lot of people used it.

Today, Alice was first to pick up her bag, and go. She did not look or speak to anyone.

'Probably got a man waiting outside,' Sandra said.

'I doubt it.'

'Why? Anyway, she's OK, quite nice really. Not easy coming in when we all know each other.'

'She certainly works hard.'

Jackets went on, scarves round necks, mirrors out to check lipstick and eye shadow.

'I think we're all agreed aren't we? Good new member of the team?'

Dilys, patting powder on her face, tying her silk scarf in a careful knot, did not reply.

'What's wrong?'

'There's just – something about her.'

We went down the stairs together. I said, 'I've known you get "feelings" about people before. So what was it?'

'It was when I bent over to help her with the key-board ...'

'What?'

She stopped and looked as if she was about to say

something, but then thought better of it and just ran on ahead of me and out of the front door.

Alice Baker said little, worked hard and left the moment the clock struck five. I think most of us liked her well enough, in so far as we knew her. When it was someone's birthday, she chipped in willingly for the usual cake and modest present. It was only odd that when Margaret asked when her birthday was, so that she could put her in the calendar, she twice seemed not to hear – at least, she did not volunteer a date. Only Dilys still did not care for her, though she never said anything nasty. But one day, when she and I went down to the bus stop together, I asked her what it was about Alice that she disliked.

'I don't dislike her. There's just something a bit off-putting. Look at that coat in Marshall's window! Not sure it's my colour though, but it would suit you.'

'What do you mean by "off-putting"? Don't change the subject.'

Dilys looked at me and her expression was – I'm not sure how to describe it exactly, but the word 'uneasy' seems to fit.

'Have you been close to her?'

I said that as my desk was on the other side of

the room, I had not, except maybe in the tea trolley queue and even then I didn't recall it. 'Why?'

'I wish that bus would hurry. I'm cold.'

It was not a cold afternoon, so she was clearly just trying to change the subject again. I just stared her out.

'All right … there's an odd smell around her.'

'What, you mean a BO smell?'

'No. I don't know what it is but it's very off-putting. Like I said.'

'Has anyone else noticed it?'

'I don't know.'

'Maybe something on her clothes.'

'Maybe.' But she looked doubtful. 'The smell hovers around her though. Still, I went to the stationary cupboard directly after her yesterday and I didn't notice anything at all then.'

'There you are – it was probably something she was wearing one day and not the next. You know how you can get an awful smell from some fabric if it gets even a bit damp.'

'Thank goodness for that, the bus at last.'

So I let the subject drop when we got to our seats.

The following day, I made it my business to go close to Alice Baker's desk, putting my hand on the door handle as if to go out, and then hesitating for a moment. I even leaned in slightly, making her glance up. She said nothing, and there was no smell of any kind around her.

And so the office days went on as usual until, one Friday evening a month later, my phone rang just after eight-thirty. It was Brenda, the office co-ordinator, to say that she felt unwell and had left an important file at work, one that she needed to read and report on by first thing the following Monday. Brenda lived a few streets from me and of course I said that I would fetch it.

'I'll leave my set of master keys in the milk box. I don't want you to come in and catch any germs from me.'

The old building was in a side street near the canal – once, I think there were wharves and warehouses, when the canal had brought barges carrying coal and pig iron and other goods into the heart of the city. They were long gone of course, though further out, where the canal flowed into the country, holiday boats chugged slowly up and down during the spring and summer, but none of these ever came into the city. Why would they? It was dirty and derelict down here, empty apart from a couple of office buildings like ours, and a few cafés and corner shops in the adjacent streets. Rubbish blew up and piled into the gutters, and oil and mud left a slick on the surface of the black canal water. The pubs had long gone.

I had taken Don's car, and I drove down the narrow street and stopped right outside the front door. The evening was drawing in and the last rays of the sun were setting behind the tower blocks on the skyline. Once, these old black roofs had been the highest in the city.

There was a low-wattage overhead bulb above the front door and another inside the hall, both of which were lit, but otherwise I had to press the switches as I went up. I had never been inside the building after hours, and certainly not alone. There were shadows and dark corners, and I did not attempt to use the black hole of a lift. But I was not alarmed by hearing only my own footsteps going up the stairs, nor by the strange quietness of a building usually full of people.

I reached the first landing. Closed doors on either side. I stopped. I had not heard or seen anything and I was not frightened of being here by myself. But something was troubling me and, after a moment, it began to take over both my mind and body and all of my senses. I felt as if I were dissolving, or perhaps

ALICE BAKER

shrivelling. I was not faint or light-headed. I had
a feeling that I was decaying. It is the only way I
can describe it. I was becoming old and I was dying,
slowly. Oxygen was giving out, though I could still
just breathe, but when I did, the air smelled noxious.
I had a sensation of creeping flesh and of things
squirming beneath my feet. Everything was being
absorbed into this horrible disintegration – the walls
and stairs, the doors and the ceiling, the light fit-
tings, the floor. And my own body. There seemed
to be not only no clean air but no hope, no future,
nothing joyous or pleasant left in existence. I was becoming mould. I looked at the backs of my hands
and they were a greenish-white, with a bloom like
the surface of mushrooms which have begun to turn.
It was a terrifying, horrible sensation, and I could
not get away from it or struggle out of it. How long
I stood on the stairs in its grip I do not know – it felt
like eternity but I actually think it was only a fleet-
ing second. Time had expanded and contracted and
I was totally confused.

And then I came to, like a diver surfacing from
black, greasy depths. I was not in the sunlight or the
clear crystal air but just where I had been, on the
staircase in the empty office block, Brenda's keys in
my hand.

I took a cautious step up, and another. The whole sensation had left me. I felt normal. Solid. Dull. Human.

I was passing our own office, when I hesitated. It should have been in complete darkness but there was a faint glimmer coming from under the door, not so much a light as a phosphorescence, but as I stared, it faded – or rather, it did not exactly fade or grow dimmer. It was simply no longer there.

When I reached the top of the next flight of stairs, I stopped dead. Ahead of me was a short corridor, with management offices on either side, and ending in a blank wall. The wall was not dark, as it should have been, but seemed to be lit from above. And it was not blank. A shadow was visible against it, entirely unmoving, like a cut-out silhouette. Someone was in the building with me. But the shadow did not flicker and the silence was so deep it was as if my ears had been stuffed with felt.

I found Brenda's office and went in, and I did not turn my back to the door as I looked for the file but went into the empty room sideways, looking behind me.

Nothing happened.

My own footsteps echoed through the building as

I ran down the stairs. The gleam under the door of my own office was there again and stronger, a white light with a faintly greenish tinge. And now, there was a faint sound from inside. My mouth went dry. I had no reason to go into the office. I had the file Brenda needed. I could leave the building quickly, lock the door and drive away. I hesitated, bending slightly towards the door. Nothing. The light had gone again. I had imagined all this.

I think of myself as a strong person, and now, perhaps foolishly, I challenged myself to check that there was no one in our own office. I put my hand out and it seemed that before I had even touched the handle, the door fell open suddenly, so that I only just saved myself from falling inwards.

Alice Baker stood there. Her expression was odd, not startled or guilty at being caught where she had no reason or right to be, at this time in the evening, but as I remembered it the day she had arrived – blank. Her eyes were not focused on me, or on anything in the office, nor even on something distant, or in her own thoughts. It was as if they were focused on – nothing at all. She stared at me for a second, and then smiled quite calmly.

'Hello.'

'Alice? What are you doing?'

She did not reply. 'Come on, I'll let us both out.'

I waited. And as I waited, I felt as if my skin and then my flesh were growing cold and damp: it was like, but not exactly like, having a sweat. I dared not touch any part of me with any other part – put my hand to my brow, for example, because I was sure that if I did I would feel – this is horrible – my flesh flake and crumble away from my bones. A weight seemed to be pressing down on me, growing heavier and heavier, suffocating me. The office had gone. I was standing in darkness. I could sense Alice Baker's presence but I could not see her. I smelled her though, a smell of mould and rottenness and decay, as if I had stumbled into an ancient cellar.

And then the sensation was gone and I was standing in the office, holding Brenda's file. From outside, I heard a church clock strike nine.

Alice Baker was no longer there.

The following day, I went in early. I needed to go up the stairs and into our office before the place filled up. I was in there for twenty minutes alone and there was nothing. No smell, no greenish light, no sense of anyone else in the room.

I had taken the file straight to Brenda's house the previous night, and as I drove home, I felt perfectly normal, though perhaps a little odd, as one feels on waking suddenly from an unpleasant dream. But the sensation faded and by the time I went to bed, it had shredded away and dissolved so that I could barely recall what had happened. If it had happened.

I was at my desk when the others came in. Alice Baker slipped into her place as usual, without speaking to anyone. And that would have been that, had it not been for the tea trolley. Two different women shared the trolley run, and this morning it was Avril, the cheerful, chattier one. The trolley stopped and office doors opened, people fetched purses, there was the usual hum of eleven o'clock and the smell of the tea urn drifting along the corridor. But as I got near, alongside Ann, whose desk was next to mine, there was a shriek and we saw that Avril was standing back, hand on her heart, face white. She was making little soft panicky noises in her throat.

When she had been calmed down and someone was making her a sugary tea, she managed to say that she had bent to pick up a bag of teacakes from the bottom of the trolley, and as she had done so, her hand seemed to go right through it, to a spongy, clinging mass inside. It was slimy, she said, cold and damp and also moving about somehow, like yeast proving or the seething scum on the surface of a stagnant pond. Various helpful explanations were offered. The bag was an old one, which had been overlooked and left there for days. In that case, someone else pointed out, the buns would have been stale and very dry.

Mice had got into the bag. In that case, the buns would have been crumbly, with holes in them. I noticed that Alice was standing to one side and very still, just watching. An accounts clerk was bending over the trolley and lifting up the bag of buns from the bottom. As they came into sight people shrank back slightly, not catching one another's eye. The bag was opened and the teacakes tipped out. They were fresh, plump, nicely browned on top, with a shiny glaze.

'There must be another bag down there then.' The accounts clerk searched all three shelves of the trolley, and then opened the door of the metal cupboard and looked inside. Unopened packs of plastic cups and lids. Bags of plastic spoons. A box of wrapped sugar cubes. Nothing else.

By this time, people were restless. Clearly Avril had had some sort of a 'turn' – perhaps she had put her hand on the wet cleaning sponge with which she wiped down. She looked tearful and embarrassed although she was still pale, but she pulled herself together and started to pour out teas.

I hung at the back until everybody else had been served and had gone. Avril looked at me.

'It's all right,' I said, 'You're not going mad.'

She was making the trolley ready to take up to the next floor and did not look at me.

'Something did happen,' I said.

'As sure as God is my witness.' Her voice was a whisper and I think the words were meant as much for herself as for me.

'Don't worry about it.'

She nodded, and was off, the trolley wheels screeching down the corridor. I have no idea what she was thinking, or how my words, which were meant as some sort of reassurance, might have been taken.

Alice Baker's head was bent over her work but as I passed, Dilys glanced up. I shrugged. I had decided not to tell her about my visit to the office the previous night. She could become slightly hysterical and the last thing we needed was an atmosphere of vague panic which would spread like a virus and have a dozen people off sick or even giving in their notice. We were short-staffed as it was. More people would come, once we were in the new building, or so we were told every so often – though I think we had all ceased to believe in that.

It was Esther's birthday on the Friday after the tea trolley incident, and as was our tradition, we all stopped work at three o'clock to present the cake and give our present – in Esther's case, a new purse. She cut the cake and the slices were handed out on paper plates. We had been gathered round Esther's desk – all except for Alice Baker, who carried on working, head down, as if nothing else was happening. She ignored her cake.

I don't know why it was this particular incident that made Dilys lose her temper and it was rather embarrassing when she marched up to Alice's desk and said 'If you don't want that, someone else will be glad to eat it.'

Alice looked up briefly at Dilys, and down again.

'Don't you like us? What have we done to deserve you, sulking in your corner? What is *wrong* with you?'

I put my hand on Dilys's arm, and Esther said, 'Never mind, leave it, just leave it,' and started to clear up the paper plates. But Dilys went on, her voice rising higher and her face going redder as she laid into Alice about how unfriendly, how peculiar, how downright nasty she was.

'Why did you come here at all? And anyway, where did you come from? I suppose they got sick of you and made your life so unpleasant you had to leave. What happened?'

Alice simply ignored her and carried on working. Dilys had to give up. It was a miserable half hour, and poor Esther, the birthday girl, was in tears.

I had never heard Alice talk about anything to do with her life – family, home, previous jobs – which was unusual. We all talked a lot about our lives outside the office. Alice Baker had been here for several months now and we none of us knew a thing about her.

I woke in the middle of the next night and for some reason I could not get rid of the unpleasant smells and sensations that seemed to be stirred up around Alice Baker, and the overwhelming sense of decay and death I had when she was near. I lay awake for a long time worrying, but I had no explanation and in the end I put it all down to my nerves. I probably needed a tonic.

A whisper went round a month later that several meetings were being held for managers and departmental heads. People scuttled into rooms which had notices pinned on their doors – CONSULTATION IN PROGRESS.

The usual rumours flew round the building, about

redundancies and downsizing, made more alarming because no one in the office had any actual facts.

When we arrived for work the following Friday, there was an envelope on every desk. People picked them up, turned them over. Put them down again. Nobody looked at anyone else. It went very quiet.

Alice Baker said, 'I know what the letters are about.'

Though we saw that hers was still unopened like the rest.

'We're moving to new offices in a month's time. The building is in Chamberlain Street.'

Dilys shot her a look of dislike. Kathleen muttered to me that somebody had a back door into management. I made a big show of ripping open my envelope and unfolding the letter. It was as she had said and it was rather funny how we all managed to make cheerful, optimistic and surprised remarks about the move and ignore Alice Baker and her prior knowledge. She had her head down working as usual, but when I glanced at her sideways just once, I saw a smile hovering on her lips. I could not work out what it meant but I felt it to be unpleasant.

At the end of that afternoon, Dilys and I were packing our things up when she put a hand on my arm to hold me back. Alice Baker was slipping out ahead of us, on her own as usual.

'I followed her the other day. She never says anything about herself. We've no more idea about her home life or where she lives now than when she arrived.'

'I suppose we don't have any right to know, really, do we? I think she's just one of those very private people.'

'She is weird.'

We started down the stairs. 'Listen. I followed her up the street. She turned left at the top and crossed the road.'

'Oh honestly, Dilys, what were you expecting to find out? That's stalking.'

'Of course it isn't.'

'Well what were you going to do, get on her bus and off at her stop and walk behind her all the way home?'

'I didn't get the chance.'

'Good'

I did not care for Alice Baker and some peculiar things had happened around her, but I thought all this was quite unnecessary.

'I didn't get the chance because she crossed the road, but before she got to the opposite pavement, she disappeared.'

'What, behind a parked car or a waiting bus or something?'

'No. She just – wasn't there any more.'

I almost laughed. I would have laughed, I think, but I saw Dilys's expression and the laugh did not come. She looked frightened.

'I mean it,' she said. 'I can't stop thinking about it. I've gone over and over what might have happened – I mean, some normal explanation. There's got to be one, hasn't there?'

There had, of course, but every one I thought of did not satisfy her, so I made an excuse and said I was going into town, not catching my usual bus.

I did make a doctor's appointment though, but when I went, everything I had planned to say about nightmares, and hallucinations to do with vile smells and strange lights under the doors of empty rooms and … well, obviously, I could not possibly come out with any of it. Either the doctor would have laughed at me or sent me for psychiatric reports. So I just said I had been feeling a bit overwrought and was sleeping badly. She said I was run-down and recommended a holiday.

And that was that.

The next three weeks were pandemonium. Everything had to be sorted out, rubbish thrown away, necessary paperwork boxed up, our personal desk drawers cleared, things labelled according to a particular system and only that system. There was no time for any daftness or imaginings and Alice Baker worked as hard as the rest of us, though she never chatted. She was very methodical, so we left the labelling system entirely to her and I must say she did it brilliantly. It was uncanny, the way she worked it all out ahead and then just did it, almost as if she had done the whole thing before. She said she understood the layout of the new building and where our section would be and that we would be more open-plan and less a little sealed-off box of our own. She obviously did have access to someone in management and got titbits of information from them, though we never saw her with anyone. But then, she could have been married to the managing director for all we knew.

A few days before we were due to move in, we were all taken on a tour of the new building, section by section. I remember how everyone was rather giggly and fluttering a bit as we walked there in a gang, rather as we had been as children when going to look at 'big school'. I found myself beside Alice for part of the way. She wore a funny knitted jacket which I thought she must have got in a charity shop because it gave off that not altogether pleasant smell that clothes from those places often do. I was surprised she went to one, to be honest, but then I knew nothing of her personal circumstances. She might have elderly parents or several children to support on her own. I felt rather sad, then, that she did not befriend any of us or join in any of our conversations about home and our family doings. It might have made her seem less odd.

The offices took our breath away. Probably in a year's time they would have become familiar as our place of everyday work and we would take them for granted, but today, the lightness and brightness of the large rooms, the sense of spaciousness, made us look forward to inhabiting them. I felt a strong sense of release and I realised how long I had worked in the dark, dingy old building and how it must have lowered my spirits, without my even knowing it. Probably all the unpleasantness of the past weeks, all my nightmares and weird imaginings, were a result of a sort of staleness, even a badness, in the cramped rooms, where little daylight ever penetrated.

We worked out the lie of the land in the new place, saw where we would be working and how the new arrangement would apply to each of us. I thought I would not want to be too close to a window, in spite of loving the light airy feel, until someone pointed out that the blinds had not yet been fitted. Nobody was going to have to work in a glare from the sun, and the windows were all double-glazed, to keep out noise and chill. I think every one of us was buoyed up by the visit. We had never really believed the move would happen.

We walked away from the old offices without a backward glance. In my imagination, I bundled together all the unpleasant experiences I had had there in recent weeks, every last thought and sensation and fear and nightmare, and dumped them down the disposal chute. My head felt clear, as if fresh light and air had been let into it. And then, I walked out of the door.

I linked everything that had happened around Alice Baker with the old offices, too. There was nothing very logical about that. It was just that they were so dark and decrepit that they seemed a likely setting for any sort of strangeness. 'Spooky' was a word most people had applied to that building at some time or other, though of course we had tried not to talk about it. We had to work there every day.

We were all looking forward to a new start. Yet the moment we had settled in, things got worse. There was a permanent, albeit faint, smell of ancient drains and the closer one got to Alice Baker the stronger the smell, either that one or another, the smell of something that had died a few weeks earlier. I once followed her down the stairs and another bad smell hung about ... like rotten eggs. Glances were exchanged but we could not mention it openly, because Alice was always there, head down, working away.

There was a sense of fear too. I began to feel it not just in the office but from the moment I woke, and it increased, until, as I neared the building, I was in a sweat of panic. Several times, I was on the point of fleeing home.

Other people had switched desks or tried to turn their chairs around, and several people who had excellent attendance records had taken sick days.

The terrible sense that the world was decaying around us came and went. Some days were quite normal, the atmosphere was pleasant and fresh. At those times, we all looked out of the big windows frequently, and, if it was not raining, took our breaks outside. Even the waste ground leading down to the canal seemed pleasant.

On one particular day, though, the air inside the office was foul and outside the sky was heavy, with bulbous clouds, tinged yellow. We felt oppressed, and people complained of headaches, as if the barometric pressure had dropped prior to a massive thunderstorm. I kept making typing mistakes, a thing I rarely do. Angela dropped her coffee mug and although the office floor had a rubberised surface, the china still shattered. The photocopier malfunctioned, the lights occasionally flickered, went off and then came on again. There was a peculiar sensation beneath our feet, a warmth, as if the office had underfloor heating. But it did not, and in any case this was August. The warmth seemed to buzz, too, if that does not sound unduly peculiar.

We had a meeting after another week of this sort of thing, and Yvonne and I were nominated to go and see Personnel.

'Is this an urgent matter? We're rather busy.'

'Yes. It is. Very urgent.'

So they slipped us in and we sat in front of a teenager – though of course she could not have been. She listened, and after a while a smirk came over her face.

'It is actually not funny. It is extremely disturbing. If you had to work in …'

'Hold on. I'll have to have a word with Mrs Kirby.'

So we were moved up to the next level. Mrs Kirby did not smirk, she sat, looking down at her desk, listening carefully.

'Is that all?' she said.

I had vowed in advance that I would not be flustered, but somehow her tart manner and expression of disapproval made me go red and I stumbled over my words.

'Well ... yes ... really ... yes. Isn't it, well, you know, enough?'

She was silent for a moment, looking at me – not at Yvonne, just at me. Yvonne might as well not have been there at all, actually, because she had not spoken, apart from to say 'Good Morning', twice.

'I think the best I can do is let the construction team know.'

'The ...'

'They're on hand for another couple of months, in case we have teething troubles in the new building. And there have been some. It's most likely a drain.'

'No, you don't understand ... it isn't there. I mean, it is ONLY there when she is in the office.'

'Which must mean all of the time ... Miss Baker has a spotless attendance record.'

'Yes, but...'

She stood up. 'As I say, the team will come and do an assessment. If there is a drain problem, or something like that, I have every confidence that they will locate it.'

'And if they don't?'

'I am quite sure they will.'

And we were out of the door and the door had closed behind us in that single smooth movement at which people in management always seem expert.

We crept back to our office and gave vague replies to all enquiries. But at the end of that afternoon, Deirdre gestured that I should stay behind and then she handed me a business card. It advertised, in quite discreet wording, the services of a Psychic.

'I think you should go. I know two people who went and she was very accurate about things she couldn't possibly have known and couldn't have guessed. I think this whole thing has gone far enough and nobody seems able to provide an explanation. What do you think?'

'Will you come with me?'

But she said she couldn't; such things bothered her. So I rang and made an appointment to go alone.

I was quite nervous. The house was ordinary enough, but there was a strange object in the window and the curtains were drawn. At first I thought the woman who opened the door was a lodger or someone of that sort. I don't know what I expected a psychic to look like, but certainly not like this, with dyed blonde hair, newly set, and a lot of bright lipstick. She wore a fluffy angora jumper and very high heels, and a lot of gold bracelets and pendants.

The room was half-dark. There was a card table at which she sat, having offered me the chair opposite. No crystal balls or anything like that. She had Tarot cards which she shuffled very fast. At first, she just spread them out and looked at them for a while, but then she said I was to ask her one question to get her started. I didn't know how to put it but eventually I just said, 'We – the people in my office and myself – we have a colleague who ... we want to know if there's something funny.'

It was not a question and it sounded stupid but she just nodded.

'Her name? Just her first name.'

'Alice.'

'And what is it that seems "funny"?'

The room smelled of candle wax and some sort of incense. It took a bit of getting used to but it didn't really bother me, and there was nothing unpleasant in the atmosphere. Nothing at all. I started to talk then, even though she hadn't indicated that I should. I told her about the feelings I had had, the awful sensations of decay and that I was dying, or dissolving. And the smells around Alice Baker, and the oddness.

She sat very still and stared at the cards, and listened. I thought I would have felt foolish but she seemed as if she had heard all this sort of thing before, and worse. She asked where Alice had come from and when, and then about the old offices and the new ones. All the time she was looking at the cards but not touching them.

I told her what I knew. There was a scratching at the door at this point and she got up to open it. A tabby cat came in. I don't care for cats, or the way they stare, but this one ignored me, got onto the window ledge, and settled down in a patch of sunlight.

'He knows,' the psychic said. 'If he doesn't like a client, doesn't like the feel of them, he won't come near this room. But you're all right.'

'It isn't really me though, is it? I mean, this isn't about me.'

'Isn't it?'

'You think it's me? Me and not her? But some of the others ...'

'I don't know what to think.'

'Oh.'

Then she swept up the cards and put them back in a pack. 'I can't give you anything. Of course there's no charge.'

'What do you mean?'

'I mean, you have come here and you are what I call completely blank. White-out. Nothing. If Alice came to me now, it might be a different story. Shall I tell you what I would do in your shoes?'

'I wish you would.'

'Find someone who does places, buildings, ground.'

'You mean – like a diviner?'

'Not exactly. Someone who will go round everywhere and see what it says to him – it's usually a man, in that line, I don't know why that should be.'

'Where would I find that sort of person? I don't know anyone who ... well, I came to you because someone recommended you.'

'They do. Which is always welcome. Personal reference. Yes.'

'So you don't know one of these men?'

I noticed that her eyes were startlingly blue, almost artificially blue. Bright, bright blue. They mesmerised me for a few seconds and gave me a strange sensation, of being seen into, and judged but not found wanting. It was almost a comforting feeling.

I left. I would never find the type of person she suggested. It seemed better to let the whole thing drop. And anyway, I knew it was all to do with Alice Baker. Anyone could tell that.

The following week, we were driven mad from the moment we arrived by the noise of pneumatic drills, and then by heavy vehicles grinding slowly past the building before tipping out loads of rubble. Even though the windows were not open it was difficult to concentrate, but eventually Brenda came in and said that this part of the work should be over today or tomorrow. They were starting on the new canteen block, which ought to have been completed at the same time as the rest of the buildings but for some reason had not even been started. Meanwhile, the old offices were being demolished.

'I'm afraid you'll have to grin and bear it, but think how nice it will be to have a proper canteen facility, even if we are sharing it with another firm.'

The noise went on until four o'clock and then stopped suddenly, leaving us with a temporary ringing in our ears, and afterwards, a wonderful quietness. The demolition was on the other side, of course. We just heard the thump of the hammer as it swung against a wall, and then a crash and a rumble. But those workmen stopped on the dot of four as well.

'All right for some.'

'Well, they're men aren't they?'

There were plenty of comments like that.

As I left, I was behind Alice Baker, who held the door for me. She glanced round as she did so, and I was startled to see her face – she looked ill, her complexion ashen and her eyes strangely sunken.

'Alice – do you feel all right?'

But she had gone.

Nothing happened for the next few days except that Alice looked more ghastly and the smell got worse and the noise from the building sites never stopped. There was also a heatwave around that time, and as the windows did not open, and several of the blinds would not work, we sweltered. In the end, so many people throughout the building complained that they sent workmen round with sheets of brown paper that they taped to the glass. It cut the glare of the sun but it didn't make the room any cooler.

On my way to the cloakroom, I passed Alice Baker's desk. She looked even more ill, grey, with huge eyes and as if the skin had been stretched more tightly over the bones of her face. I noticed that she had on a dress with long sleeves and a scarf round her neck.

'Aren't you boiling?'

She lifted her head but did not look directly at me. That was always the way.

'I feel the cold.'

'So do I. When it is cold. It's sweltering today, hadn't you noticed?' But her head was bent over her work again.

Just after eleven o'clock that morning the noise of the machinery stopped suddenly. Often, one side or the other might go quiet or there would be no lorries for a while, but there had not been a time until now when it all ceased early in the day. It was uncanny. But after looking up, or remarking, we all simply got back on with our work and thought no more about it. Two other things happened. When I went past Alice Baker's desk at ten to five, it was empty. The chair was tucked in and the surface was cleared. Perhaps she had felt ill and gone home early, but nobody who worked near her had been aware of anything. She must have just slipped out. That was unsurprising. Alice was always very private in her behaviour, but she was also quite a considerate person and if she had been unwell she would not have wanted to make a fuss and disturb the rest of us.

It was still very hot. The whole of the canal site

was dry and baking and a hot little wind swirled patches of dust and sand and rattled the stalks of the tall weeds by the fence. The lorries had gone. The demolition site was empty of both machinery and men. The new canteen block was roofless under the sun.

The only explanation I could think of was either that it was too hot to work, the building firm had gone bankrupt, or there was a strike – perhaps because it was too hot to work. Well, we were in the same boat. I had actually felt quite faint and sick in the middle of the day, from the airlessness and heat of our office, but it had not occurred to anyone to walk out. What I actually did, because I had an even bigger workload than usual, and, as Head of Section I couldn't delegate any of it, was ring Brenda.

'I agree it was pretty intolerable today. Personnel seem to be powerless as ever.'

'What I wonder is, can I go in early, get as much done as possible while it's cool and the sun is on the other side – and then leave earlier?'

'I would be happy with that,' Brenda said, 'but I don't think it could be extended to everyone else. Still, if you felt sick and as you do have a lot on your plate ...'

'I can be in at six.'

Brenda groaned. 'Of course the system has changed now. I don't have a full set of keys any longer, but the night security man is on until seven, he'll let you in. Make sure you take your identity pass.'

We had certainly come bang up to date at our place.

It was a soft, milky morning, and the streets were cool. I was in the offices by five-thirty. The night security man looked as if I had woken him up, which, if true, was not right at all. It was cool in the building too, cool and quiet. There was an odd sense of tranquillity, which I had never experienced during working hours. I settled down at my desk and in an hour I had done as much as I would normally manage in two, what with interruptions, and the heat and the general coming and going – not to mention the noise outside. There was none of that either. The machinery was still shut down, and the site deserted.

I took a break after another half hour, to stretch and move my neck and shoulders, and then to go to the cloakroom. As I opened the office door onto the corridor I heard footsteps. They were soft and seemed to be the footsteps of someone running, pattering along as a dog patters. I waited but no dog appeared, and nor did any person.

When I came out of the cloakroom, I heard the steps again, but as I stopped, they stopped. And then, at the far end of the corridor, I saw a child. It was a small child, perhaps four or five years old, though it was shadowy and hard to tell if it was a boy or a girl – yet strangely, I knew instinctively that it was a girl; I was quite certain of it. She wore a pale garment, a dress or a nightdress and, at first she stood absolutely still and just looked at me. I shivered, but I was not afraid. I knew that this was not a real child. That was the other certainty. I was looking at a ghost. A real living child could not possibly be in the building alone at this time. But my assurance of her ghostliness had nothing to do with this sort of reasoning. It was just a kind of 'knowledge'.

I did not know whether to leave or go, move or speak, or stay still. But then the child began to beckon to me, lifting her arm slowly. I was to go to her. I began to walk forwards, without any hesitation, any alarm, but as soon as I moved the child moved, went ahead, still beckoning. I followed her up the stairs, along the corridor past all the closed doors, up the next staircase, and the next. On the top floor there was a single door. 'FIRE EXIT.' I knew that it led out onto a balcony, railed in and leading to a fire escape, and was only to be used by those on the top two floors. It had a green light above it and could only be opened by pressing an emergency bell which was beside me on the wall. Once a week the bell was tested, along with all the other fire alarms throughout the building. We knew to put our hands over our ears.

The bell had not sounded and the escape door was closed. There was no one here. The child could not have opened the door without sounding the alarm which was, in any case, at adult not child height. I did not think she could have reached it. I listened. Nothing. No footsteps. Nothing.

I started back down the flights of stairs but again I heard the steps, behind me. I looked back. Waited. Nothing.

I went on. I was not in the least afraid of this small pattering ghost, though I could not imagine why she was haunting the place or where she belonged.

There had not been a building on this part of the site before; it had been waste ground. All the buildings had been on the side of our old offices.

I returned to my desk and settled back to work, only to find that I had run out of typing paper. We kept a small supply of stationery in a cupboard in our office but there were no boxes of paper left. Which meant a trip down to the basement. That room had everything in bulk and, as Head of Section, I held a key.

The night security guard would still be on duty but he was not in his box. It was not quite seven o'clock and presumably he did a last round of the building around now. I wondered if he would see the little girl.

From the ground floor down there were wall lights permanently switched on, and they gave off a rather cold, bluish light. The rest of the building still smelled of new wood, paint and flooring, but down here it smelled of cement dust and staleness. I reached the basement corridor and it hit me like the force from a powerful gust of wind, though everything around me was still. What I felt was a terrible dread and fear, a nightmarish sense that something terrible had happened, or was going to happen. I remembered feeling this weeks before but I had been fine and apparently well-balanced since so I was shocked when my legs almost gave way. But there was no one about, the lights were on, the doors were closed – even the little girl had not pattered all the way down here. And *she* had not given me the faintest sense of unease.

I did not want to stay down here. I wanted to fly back up to the light and apparent safety of the floors above, but I steeled myself and walked down the corridor to the office supplies room. As I went, I felt as if I were being suffocated or strangled, and an awful coldness came over me. My skin felt damp, and my head was pounding, as if the blood was struggling through the veins.

I needed to tell someone but there was no one to tell. I needed help but help was elsewhere. I stopped, took several shuddering deep breaths and forced myself to the door of the room, key ready, though I had to try two or three times to turn it because I was shaking and my palm was clammy. Why I felt like this I had no idea but now I had a surge of annoyance with my own stupidity and in a moment of strong resolve I turned the key and opened the door. There was no switch, the light came on automatically, and in that light, I saw, and then I screamed and I heard my own screams echoing along the basement corridor, and at last, at last, I also heard the sound of a man's footsteps, plunging down the stairs.

I stood, my hand up to my mouth, staring at the swinging figure. Alice Baker had hanged herself from the metal girder that ran across the ceiling.

I held onto consciousness until the night security

guard reached me and then I lost it and crumpled at his feet.

They talked of sending me into a hospital which, they said, would help me to recover because I would have intensive therapy in 'a safe environment'. But I felt safe at home. I could not have gone to work: even if I had been capable of doing my job I did not think I could ever enter that building again. But being quiet, sedated just enough to make me relaxed and calm, was right for me. I slept late, I pottered about, I read a lot – gentle, undemanding books. I started knitting again. I looked at magazines. Friends and neighbours and relatives came and brought food and drink and stayed to chat. And Don was lovely to me, though I think he was very glad he did not have to spend the whole day at home. He loved his work, and when he got back he was tired but glad to cook, to chat to me and cheer me up. And so it went on for several months. I was not supposed to talk about anything that had happened, except to the psychiatrist I saw. But she sat and said nothing and frowned and seemed to have no interest in me. She asked me nothing. She made no remarks. She wrote a few notes, but I think I was expected to do all the work while she got paid. I stopped seeing her after a short time. In any case, I knew I didn't need someone like that. I needed time and space and peace and quiet.

I got all of those things and I began to feel steadier and to be able to work out, bit by bit, what had happened and what had not. Alice Baker had happened. The night I saw her in the old office building had happened. Hadn't it? Had it? All the things that had surrounded her and emanated from her, those were real enough – all the girls from the office who came to see me confirmed that all right. They had experienced everything and not one was in any doubt.

Two things were troubling, to me and to everyone else. No one had ever seen the ghostly child, or heard her pattering feet. The one person most likely to have done so, the night security guard, denied any sighting of her, or, indeed, any encounter of a supernatural nature, during his time on duty. He left the job shortly after coming to my rescue. But before he went, he absolutely denied that there had been anyone – not Alice Baker, or any other – hanging in the office supplies room. When he found me, almost unconscious, he had glanced into the room, checked and then closed the door. He had assumed that I had just opened it with my key when I had been taken ill. When I came round, not long afterwards, he said that I had been babbling about something, someone, about Alice, about someone swinging from the girder and then about a little child on the top floor, vanishing through the fire escape door. He had re-alised that I was delirious or in a deranged mental state. He had even gone back and checked in case he found the slightest evidence of someone having been in the office supplies room, or on the top floor … he had found nothing.

There was no body. There had not been a body. No one had hanged themselves, not Alice Baker or any other employee. There had been no small girl. That was the most unlikely thing of all; and no one believed me, even when I described her. The fact that Alice Baker did not come in to work that day, or ever again, did not convince anyone that she had done anything other than walk out without notice.

'She was always a bit odd.' That was the general opinion. No one mentioned the things that had sur-rounded her, the weird smells, the sense that some-thing bad was about to happen. Perhaps people felt they would be associating themselves too closely with my own 'mental breakdown' and so they con-veniently forgot everything. One or two from the office came to see me but if I mentioned Alice Baker or anything connected with what had happened, I saw their expressions change, and they looked away from me. After a time, they stopped coming.

I felt well again in quite a short time. I was able to live a normal everyday life. But if I thought of returning to work, I was overcome with panic. Don said I should resign, on health grounds. He said I could probably get some sort of pay-off for the shock and distress but I doubted that and I have plenty of pride. I would not have dreamed of asking for a thing.

There was no hurry. Don brings in a good salary and we have no family. I would just look in the local newspaper for something that might suit. It was there that I saw it.

In the midst of seeing the small girl, or not seeing her, and finding Alice Baker hanged, or not finding her, I had completely forgotten about that last day when all the machines and lorries had ground to a halt and all the builders disappeared. Now, I saw on the front page a photograph of the whole site, with people in hard hats and a lot of trenches dug in lines and marked out with posts and tape.

I started to read the article below the picture but as soon as I did, the old sense of dread and horror overwhelmed me, so that I had to throw the paper aside. I sat, shaking, not understanding why it had all returned, why, after so many weeks, I was pushed back into the past, as if I had never felt any better than this. But I had, I had.

When Don came in and saw me he looked distraught. And something else. Just for a moment, he looked annoyed, impatient, as if he were blaming me, infuriated that it had all started up again, just as he believed things had returned to normal. I suppose I didn't blame him. It must be very wearying, living with someone in this state. He made a pot of tea and brought it in.

'Anything tempting in the jobs line?'

I think he wanted me to make a bit of an effort by now.

'One or two,' I said. He gave me a look, knowing what I actually meant. That I hadn't even turned to the adverts page. He picked up the paper and started to look at the photograph. I drank my tea. I had my eyes closed.

'Here, have you seen this?'

He was jabbing the page with his forefinger.

I shook my head. 'Not really.'

'Yes you have. Of course you have.'

'I glanced at the picture … some sort of earthworks going on.'

' No. It's a dig, an archaeological dig. It says it has been going on for three weeks and that …' he mumbled as he went back to the report. I didn't want to know anything. I was steadier. Calmer. I wanted to stay like that.

'Read it,' Don said, holding out the paper.

'No, I'm really not interested.'

'All right, I'm going to read it to you.'

"No …" I stood up, and shouted it. 'NO!'

But he took no notice. He just started to read.

The building works had stopped suddenly that day because the workmen had dug up a large piece of curved stone which, when they looked closely, had some lettering still visible on it. And then, looking into the scoop of the excavator, the operator had seen what he was sure was a human skull. At that point, after a telephone call, they were ordered to stop digging.

Local historians and archivists from the County Records Office have released an initial statement, confirming that it is likely to be the town's unconsecrated burial ground for those who died by their own hand or in other circumstances where a church burial was denied them. This ground has been known about for many years but several locations were suggested and investigated without success. Paul Thessaly, heading the team, confirms that several things point to this as the correct site: 'We have already found a number of graves, and

*although many cannot be identified, several do have
still-visible lettering which we have photographed and
are trying to decipher and match with any records. This
is not easy as the names of those who were buried in unconsecrated ground – and this graveyard was open until
the middle of the nineteenth century – were often not
recorded.'*

Don looked at me. I could not think why this news
had put me into such a state of trepidation. I was not
troubled by graves and cemeteries, I had no fear of
the dead. If I had sat at my desk year after year, on
top of a place where the unfortunates who had been
cast out of the church had been buried, it was not of
any consequence. Sad but not frightening.

'Shall I go on?'

'If you want to but…'

Don poured us more tea.

'I think you'll find it interesting,' he said, 'to say
the least.'

And he read that the most recent grave to be exca-
vated contained not one but two skeletons, each one
intact. They had been placed side by side with the
arm of the larger one laid round that of the smaller,
'… a woman, and a child, the latter a girl, aged
four to five years old. Marks on the neck bones of

the woman indicated that she had died by hanging, probably with some sort of heavy buckled belt. No marks were detected on the skeleton of the child.'

The flat covering stone had nothing engraved on it except the worn initials A.B. with a + sign, beside it, indicating the child, whose name had not been recorded.

THE FRONT
ROOM

One

They blamed one another for what happened but in fact it all began with Pastor Lewis's address.

The Irwins were quite regular chapelgoers, though would never have called themselves devout. It had taken them some time to settle, having moved from the Anglo-Catholic parish church to its Evangelical neighbour to non-comformist Baptist then Methodist, before settling on Pastor Lewis's small building with the corrugated roof, and finding that its particular brand of simple informality suited them best. One Saturday evening a month, there was an 'in touch' service, which they had never quite got round to attending, the word in the neighbourhood being that it was reminiscent of spiritualism. 'Perhaps a step too far?' Norman said. But there was nothing untoward about Pastor Lewis's regular Sunday worship.

The address that sparked everything off was given on a dank morning in late October, just before All Souls' Day. The chapel heaters had been switched on so that the air smelled of burning dust, but any warmth only rayed out in a semi-circle a few feet from the radiators and the fifty-odd worshippers huddled together at the edges of the benches, so as to be closest to them.

The address – Pastor Lewis did not believe in the word 'sermon' – was lukewarm to begin with, but within a few minutes had blazed up, so that everyone was touched by its fire and passion. But no one, it transpired later, had been quite so moved that they were spurred into action, like the Irwins.

The text was from Isaiah: '… to share your bread with the hungry and bring the homeless poor into your house.'

Pastor Lewis had stuttered a little, and his small eyes had gleamed, as he became more and more aroused by his own exhortations. He was a bald, rather porcine man who hid behind rimless spectacles, but oratory was his strength. People had come, dazed, out of the service and had hurried home, suddenly uncomfortable inside their own skins, heads ringing with the ferocious words.

Nothing was said until Norman Irwin had begun

to carve the joint of lamb, with its gleaming, oozing juices. Belinda set down the dishes of vegetables and then looked hard at the table.

'Plenty,' she said. 'We have "Plenty".'

Their children, Wallace and Fern, caught the solemnity as it brushed past them, and were still. Laurie banged the spoon down on the table of his high chair, with a crack that startled them. They laughed at themselves.

'Fern, cut up Laurie's meat for him please and get him started, before he does that again.' Belinda sat down.

'Bless, Oh Lord, this food for our use and us for Thy Service. Amen.'

The address had stressed that it was not necessarily a question of going out and actively looking for destitute street sleepers. 'Those in most need may be close to us, close beside us – closer than we know. Is it a next-door neighbour? Is it the old man picking through his small change in the doorway of the store, before he dares to go in? Is it an old, long-forgotten friend? We must give to those charities which support the oppressed and the homeless of this world but then look closer to ourselves, look in our own streets, our own neighbourhood. In what way can we help? What can we give? What can we share? The food on our table? A place at our fireside? Do not think small, think big, my friends, think …' He spread his arms wide, 'think VAST! May God bless you.' He held up his hands, the fingers stained yellow after forty years of cigarette smoking. (Prayer was said to have caused him to give up, snap, overnight. It was known as the Pastor's miracle.)

'Well, of course we give to charity,' Belinda said. 'Which is easy.'

'Is the point of it that it has to be hard? I'm not disagreeing with you, by the way, just wondering aloud.'

'I think he implied as much.'

Wallace and Fern cleared their plates of what they intended to eat. Wallace stuck his legs out from under the tablecloth and stared at his shoes. They were docile children.

'We are very fortunate, Norman.'

'Privileged.'

Belinda, never sure precisely what that meant, speared a slice of carrot. 'We should definitely give this some thought.'

'As a substitute for actually doing anything?'

'Not at all. No, I definitely think we should do something about it.'

'What about?' Fern said. Sly little Fern, always listening.

'Pass your plate please.'

They looked at the front room that same evening. The house was very typical, very straightforward, 1920s. Low front gate. Hedge. Small front garden, small lawn. Birdbath in the centre, which made mowing awkward. Long narrow back garden. Fence. Anyone could have gone round the interior blindfold. Hall. Large front room. Bow window. Back room, knocked out to the terrace with a flat-roof extension, done before the Irwins arrived. Kitchen. Downstairs cloakroom. Three bedrooms. Bathroom. Landing, which caught the afternoon sun. Attic. A neat house. Perfect for them.

'This is a very nice room, actually.' Norman said.

'And underused. Face it, when do we sit in here?'

'Christmas Day.'

The blue three-piece suite, inherited from Belinda's parents' front room, was still like new. They stood, each picturing a slightly different arrangement. A bed here? A modern electric fire? Or a larger radiator? Where would clothes go? Was there room for a desk? Or perhaps just a small table in the window.

'It is rather dark,' Belinda said, 'on this side of the house.'

It was dark now. Norman switched on the

overhead light, which threw shadows and somehow made things worse. The room smelled of cold and a lifeless emptiness.

That night they lay side by side, each thinking about the Pastor's address and the obligation they felt it had placed upon them. The front room. Their thoughts merged into dream states, in which different images swirled, of men sleeping in doorways beside patient dogs, women on park benches, prone bundles of grey clothing, people queuing for night shelters, with years of dirt beneath their fingernails and in the creases of their necks. Wild eyes. Muttering. Shuffling. The smell of stale drink.

The subject was not mentioned again for some days. Once or twice, Belinda stood in the doorway of the front room. Who could actually occupy a space into which the sun never shone? She went to the window. She had never realised how depressing the view was, of a grass rectangle, a stained concrete birdbath and a privet hedge. Who would be happy looking out on those all day?

Besides, there were the children. And she saw them in her mind's eye, curled up together on the sofa in the family room. They had to think of the children.

*

'Dear Norman and Belinda,' Norman read out. They had an agreement that he opened letters addressed to them both.

Well, it is not very warm for the time of year. I had the chiropodist call yesterday. I could manage to get to her office in a taxi but aren't taxis expensive? Anyway, it's nice to be done in the privacy of home. I expect the Christmas windows will be filling up before long, it seems to start earlier every year so I will send off my postal orders for the children in good time. I hope we have a mild winter. You don't want snow at my age. I don't see many people.

Well, look after yourselves,
from
Solange

The children had supper. Baths. Milk. Bed. Belinda had made a large casserole, a portion each and four for freezing. The last of their own potatoes. They didn't grow very much but always potatoes. So easy. It was Solange, years ago, who had said there was nothing like them, fresh from the ground, straight into the boiling water. But if they were both put in mind of her again now, nothing was said.

The ten o'clock news. Belinda sorted out the

children's socks. Keep. Throw. Keep. Match. Throw. Keep.

Telepathy sparked between them. 'How long since we went to see her?'

'Too long.'

'It's rather a poisonous letter, actually.'

'Is it?'

'Reading between the lines.'

Solange sidled into the room then, Solange who could never be ignored, though they had done their best for six years.

'I do feel a bit responsible,' Norman said. 'She's well over eighty.'

Norman's mother had died when he was fifteen and then it had just been Norman and Ralph, his depressed and grieving father. They had both been domestically incompetent, emotionally crippled, and with barely a trace of mutual understanding. The question of affection had never arisen, though if they had been asked, each would have claimed to love the other. They never were asked.

Norman had gone to London, to study law. When he returned at the end of his first term, Solange was already installed, like a replacement cooker, fully connected. She was already quite familiar with the ways of the house. The fact that his father had acquired a mistress who, a few months later, became a wife, did not trouble Norman. Indeed, it was a relief to his own sense of guilt, at having left Ralph alone. So, when he went home he welcomed Solange (who was English, but had had a French grandmother) who in turn welcomed him, though rather more coldly.

After university he went into the law firm with which he had remained, through several takeovers and amalgamations, and his stepmother played little part in his life. It was only after he and Belinda were engaged and he took her to meet them that he began to see the true nature of things. Solange made his father's life a misery. She treated him like a child or an idiot and always as her inferior. She was rude and overbearing, she took offence at anything, and could turn an innocent remark into a slight, usually provoking a bitter quarrel from which she apparently gained pleasure. She argued, contradicted, blamed and had sudden fits of rage, during which, lacking all grasp of reason or proportion, she lashed out at whoever was nearest, sometimes physically.

When Wallace was born, Belinda refused to allow Solange near him. After Fern came, there was a vicious letter, for no reasons they could fathom, and the rift was complete. They did not visit again. Twice, Ralph managed to come to visit them surreptitiously overnight, though fearful that somehow Solange would learn about it. The second time, Fern had been slightly sick on his shoulder and he had suffered paroxysms of anxiety, until Belinda had sprayed his jacket clean, dried and pressed it. There had been no trace left of any smear or smell but Ralph had left the house turning his neck every few minutes to check on the shoulder.

A month later he was dead. Wallace and Fern were left a hundred pounds each and Norman his father's car – Solange did not drive. The rest went to her – the rest being eleven thousand pounds and the house, in which she had lived, bitterly and alone ever since. Arthritis clamped down on her joints, isolating her even more, and her own nature did the rest.

'I can go for days without speaking to a living soul,' the letters read, 'I talk to the four walls,' and 'my neighbours are not nice people.'

Laurie was born. Belinda returned to teaching art, part time. Fern had intestinal problems and needed a special diet. Solange went to the back of their minds and letters became infrequent.

They stood in the doorway of the front room,

in silence. Belinda drew the curtains. Switched on a lamp.

'Better,' Norman said. 'It just needs a brighter bulb.'

'Get rid of the sofa, the whole room would open out.'

'And the bureau. I can't think why we wanted to keep it.'

They inspected the downstairs toilet. 'Actually,' Norman said, after tapping walls, going outside and coming back in, 'it might be simpler than you'd suppose.' He waved his arms about. Knock down. Partition. Extend. Move that pipe. New floor. Plumbing. 'A shower would fit in quite neatly.'

'Shower?'

'No room for a bath. Absolutely not.'

It took three months and rather more money than they had budgeted, but the result was pleasing. The children bounced on the new bed-settee and switched the radiant fire on and off, before being banned from the front room. Magnolia walls, dusky-pink curtains, darker pink carpet, grey cushions and covers. A new TV. Tea-maker on its own stand. Telephone point. Shower room just across the hall. At the last minute Belinda added a microwave on a special shelf, with a curtained cupboard below for crockery. They looked round and felt pleased.

Solange had not yet been invited.

'You have to go up there,' Belinda said. 'This isn't something for just a phone call or even a letter.'

'Me?'

'Well, she isn't my stepmother.'

The journey took three and a half hours. The motorways appeared to carry twice the traffic since his last visit. Perhaps it was longer ago than he remembered, after all. But he had time to think about the plan and about how Solange might fit into … where, exactly? Not their household, and certainly not their family. She was to be offered the chance to live her own life, independent of, but sheltered by, them. That sounded right. All the same, the nearer he got to his old home, the more incidents he remembered – the terrible things that had been said, her knack of twisting a happy situation into a miserable one, good intentions into bad. There were reasons why he had not been here since the new estates had been built. Much of the town he knew had gone and a ring road divided the remainder, like a tarmac river. But the house had not changed. The window frames needed replacing, the front door repairing, the gate re-painting. The porch smelled faintly of unemptied dustbins.

Solange had changed. Aged. Pink scalp showed through her now-white hair, like a joint of uncooked pork. She walked with two sticks.

'Oh, Norman, I'm so pleased to see you, I'm so glad you came. I think about you, all of you, every day. I miss you all every day. I wish I could see the children.'

Where was the old Solange? Age, isolation, illness – perhaps these had worn down the sharp corners, smoothed the rough edges. He slept in his old room, making up the bed himself because she could no longer struggle with it. He dared not ask how she changed her own.

He had brought lamb chops with him, and a lemon tart, vegetables too, in a cold bag, and he cooked them. The hobs were black with grease thick as old tar. When he lit them, acrid smoke poured out so that he had to open the door and both windows. He had brought a bottle of red wine but she said her stomach was 'beyond drink'. He washed hardened stale food off the cutlery and laid the table.

Pastor Lewis's address burned in his ears. The hungry. The poor. The homeless. Not quite, but she was old, infirm and lonely. Her daily life was a

157

struggle. He had a pain in his chest, where tears of remorse formed a hard lump.

Solange wept when he talked about it to her. He realised he had never seen her weep before.

'It's the answer to a prayer,' she said, 'the answer to a prayer, Norman.'

She wanted to be off now, tonight, it was all he could do to rein her in, prevent her from making a start on the packing. They agreed that, for the time being, she would simply close up this house and leave it. In six months, assuming that she had settled and was happy, he would come up again and put it on the market. ('And of course the money will be yours, yours and Belinda's and the children's, in return for taking me in. God bless you.') But he said that they would not dream of it.

'It's the right thing to do,' he said to Belinda. 'The right thing.'

They felt good about themselves.

She had said that of course she did not need to see the room, she knew it would be wonderful. It was going to be all she had longed for. But when she did see it for the first time she seemed taken aback.

'How do we put it to her,' Belinda had asked, 'about, you know, "house rules"?'

Their idea was that Solange would share Friday evening supper with them, and Sunday lunch every week, but cater for herself the rest of the time. Belinda was happy to drive her anywhere, in the quest to meet new people and make friends with at least some of them. She had thought vaguely of their chapel, or any other church Solange might prefer, and of the community centre, which offered classes and social groups. And, of course, these new friends must be invited back to her room, whenever it pleased her. She could book taxis to take her out when Belinda was not free. Anything she needed she would be encouraged to suggest – a DVD player, Norman thought, and they had gone out and bought an expensive radio the moment she mentioned having left hers behind.

The children were always to knock if they wanted to visit, 'Just the same as if she lived in the house next door.'

She arrived on a Friday, ate early supper with them, but then retired to the front room. They heard the radio, then the television. Slow footsteps and the flush of the toilet. The shower defeated her. 'I have baths,' she said, 'I've never had a shower in my life.'

Norman explained the workings of the shower patiently, several times, and in the end, Belinda overcame a small reluctance to help Solange into the shower, wash and get out.

'I don't know I'm sure. I can't see that I shall get used to it.'

'No,' Belinda said that night, 'I'm sorry but not our bath, there are already too many of us and also, it's a question of the stairs.'

Solange made quite a business of crossing the hall on her sticks. Hearing her breathe heavily as she shuffled, Norman had opened the living room door and offered help. She had turned on him a look of hatred, which he felt like an electric shock. She did not speak. He closed the door.

Belinda did not teach on Mondays. She dropped the children at school, tidied the kitchen, put a load of washing on, and gave Laurie his snack before putting him down for his sleep. Then, as usual, she settled down for a coffee and the paper. She had just done so, on this first Monday, when the door opened.

'Solange! Come in. Is everything all right for you? Would you like some coffee?'

Solange looked slowly round the room, eyes resting on every surface, every object, and then out of the window onto the garden, and then back to

Belinda. Hers were odd eyes, pebble-coloured with a needle of yellow at their centre.

Belinda cleared her throat. 'Do come and sit down.'

'There's a nasty draught in that room.'

'Is there? I'm sorry, Solange. I'll check your windows and if it isn't that, Norman will have a look when he gets home.'

'Nobody comes.'

'Solange, don't just stand there – talking of draughts. Come in and have coffee.'

'I can't think why you had me here. I sit on my own wondering that.'

'Well, because …'

'You never liked me. And there goes that child. Cries a lot doesn't he, that Laurie.'

'No more than any other two-year-old. He's rather a contented little boy, actually.'

'I hear them clumping up and down right over my head, clump clump, up and down.'

The effort of holding the words back made Belinda's face burn. 'Why did you call him Laurie?'

'Well, it's Lawrence, really…'

But Solange had turned away, though as she did so, Belinda saw a needle-flash of hatred from the woman's eyes that seemed to pierce her flesh with a split second of pain.

The door closed.

She decided to say nothing.

That Sunday, family lunch was uneventful, with everyone on their best behaviour until, without warning, Solange leant over Fern.

'Don't make that gobbling noise when you're eating, you disgusting little girl.'

Spittle from the venom with which she spoke caught Fern's cheek. Fern went white. Wallace ducked, fearing his turn would come next. The air crackled. Only Laurie laughed and laughed and banged his spoon. Solange picked up her knife and fork and went on eating quite calmly.

'You,' Belinda said, fighting back either tears or fury, or both. They had put on a TV cartoon for the children, an unprecedented thing on a Sunday, and were upstairs in their bedroom. 'You. She's your stepmother.'

'Yes.'

'How dare she?'

'Yes. No, I know. Awful.'

'I will not have her speak to the children like that, I will not have her correcting them.'

'Yes. No.'

She sat down on the bed. 'Fern wasn't even making a noise when she ate.'

'No.'

'This has to stop now.'

'Yes.'

The following morning, Belinda came in ten minutes earlier than usual from her school and saw that the front room door was ajar. She had wrestled with herself but in the end, wanting peace in the air, had bought Solange a small bunch of flowers.

There was no reply from her tap. She looked in. The room was empty, as was the kitchen, shower and toilet. Solange was slightly deaf, enough not to hear Belinda's quiet footsteps on the staircase.

She was sitting at the dressing table, whose drawer was hanging open and spilling its contents. She did not turn round, only stared at Belinda's reflection in the mirror, eyes gleaming.

'Please do not come into our room when we are out and please do not go through my drawers. I would not dream of doing that to yours. If you want something, ask me.'

As she was speaking, she was aware of an unpleasant smell surrounding Solange. Oh God, not that, please not that.

'I would like you to go back downstairs.'

Solange did not move. 'I am not your child to order about. And your child has been in *my* room, poking and prying.'

'I am quite sure they have not.'

'She. The girl.'

'Fern would never do such a thing.'

'The little listener. She's a sly one.'

If she had stayed there Belinda might have hit her, but Solange got up and scuttled off like a rat, without her sticks or, apparently, the need of them.

'We can't just throw her out,' Norman said, twisting his fingers together. 'Doesn't it defeat the whole point of ...'

'She is not staying here to pry into my things and malign our children.'

'I'll have a word.'

'A word won't be of any use, Solange is beyond words. She sits in there. She has made no attempt to socialise. I have offered to take her to all sorts of things, but she says she wouldn't like the people. She comes into the kitchen unannounced, she ...'

'I said I'd have a word.'

Somehow things were smoothed over, or else

brushed under the carpet and never mentioned. Somehow they sat through a Friday-night supper without unpleasantness.

A week later, in the evening, urgent, hysterical crying came from the children's room. Belinda ran up. Norman switched off the television.

Wallace was sitting up in bed, pale as dough, holding out his arm and making an odd, gulping noise. In the soft flesh above his elbow, teeth marks were swelling into a red weal. As she screamed out for Norman to come, the smell was there again, a little pocket of it in the air above Wallace's bed, foetid, rancid.

When Belinda flung herself in through the door of the front room, without knocking, she found it dark, but in the orange glow of the street lamp, through a chink in the curtains, she saw Solange in bed, and asleep, snores coming from her half-open mouth. The smell, coming from around her bed, was stronger than ever now.

'Oh God,' Belinda said, 'Oh God.'

'But where can she go?" Norman stared at the wall, desperate to be anywhere but in his own house, facing his own wife.

It was not quite the answer to a prayer when the

front door bell rang, but close to it: Pastor Lewis was on the step, although he was only delivering papers for the next meeting of the chapel council.

He accepted coffee, sat with them at the table, cigarette-stained forefingers in an arch, permanent evidence of his miracle.

'Evil,' Belinda said.

'Now evil is a very strong word.'

'I can't think of another, can you?'

'What you did was a very good thing, a good act,' he said, ducking and diving. 'Few would have taken me at my word, or rather, the Lord at his. Few ever do.'

'But no good deed goes unpunished.'

'I would never say that, never. That is to be cynical.'

'If you have no advice, Pastor …'

'Of course, I see your problem, I do see it.'

'She has to go,' Belinda said, looking him in the eyes, 'it is only a question of where.'

'And when.'

'As soon as possible, is the when.'

'But where, you know.'

'Back to her own house. Or into a home.'

'Homes have to be paid for,' Norman said, uneasy, unhappy.

Belinda stood up and banged her hand hard down on the table, so that the mugs jumped, coffee was spilled, and the door opened on Solange, leaning on her sticks, hair like a half-blown dandelion clock.

Then Pastor Lewis did an unexpected thing. 'Come, Solange,' he said leading her from the room. 'I think you and I should have a talk.'

It was two hours later, when he was running very late for all his evening appointments, that he put his head back round the kitchen door. 'I think we have an understanding,' he said, 'though I'm afraid I got nowhere with the concept of error, let alone wrongdoing. Meanwhile, praise the Lord, I hope you will find that things improve.'

'Thank you, Pastor,' Belinda said, though unconvinced. They stood on the step and she lowered her voice. 'Were you aware of a smell? A very unpleasant smell, in the front room?'

He was fidgeting to get away. 'No criticism, Belinda, none at all of anyone, but managing that sort of thing gets harder as we grow old. Perhaps, a cleaner once a week? The district nurse would advise.'

Oh God.

*

The children scuttled past the front room now, even Laurie, for the fear was contagious. Wallace's bites healed, though the bruising took a while to fade. Fern stood close to Belinda if Solange came near.

'You're welcome, any of you, at any time. I could teach you to knit, Fern.'

'I don't want to knit.'

'I could teach you to play Racing Demon.'

Fern's hands tightened round her mother's arm.

Meeting a neighbour at the gate, Belinda suggested she might like to pop in on Solange, when she herself was teaching. 'Tuesday mornings and Thursday all day. She would so appreciate some company.'

The neighbour came on the following Thursday, with an offering of cake and a bunch of pinks. She came on the Tuesday, too, though empty-handed. But not again.

'She won't want to make a habit of it and then not to be able to stick to that, it can be very disappointing, when there's an expectation.'

'There must be someone else.'

But any others there were made excuses, not meeting Belinda's eye.

'She's talked to them – Mrs Baker. Put them off.'

'Now why would she do that?'

'The same reason as she won't come again herself.'

'And that would be …?'

'Because Solange is evil.' Norman raised his eyebrows.

'They can smell it.' But Belinda did not actually say that.

Nothing else happened, except that sometimes, as Belinda went across the hall, the door of the front room was opened a chink and then closed quickly. She still came in to eat Sunday lunch with them. Her radio or TV were turned up too loudly. She left the shower running. Laurie ran up to her door and bashed on it with a wooden brick or his tractor and laughed at the rage of words coming from inside. The next time, the door opened very suddenly, and he fell flat, hitting his face, and wailed in pain and outrage. Solange turned on the radio to full volume and ignored him.

'I cannot stand it. I cannot have her in my house a day longer.'

'Our house.'

'Your stepmother.'

'I'll have a word.'

'When? When? You say that, you say it, but you have never had any word, you never see her, you avoid her, anything to save your own skin. WHEN?'

'When' was eight o'clock that evening. Solange heard him in silence. He took some time, twisting his hands together, clearing his throat.

'You do see? That it isn't working well – I mean, for you. You do understand? We are thinking of you, Solange. So … So, these would seem to be the options. Back to Linden Close. Or … a nice home.' He said it again, stressing the 'nice'. 'There. Or here, where you would still be near to us. Obviously it's entirely up to you. Obviously.'

Solange leaned forward. 'Come here, Norman. Come nearer to me.'

He moved nearer, smiling.

She spat in his face.

At three in the morning Belinda came awake like a diver surfacing fast, to a ringing in her ears and a brutal pressure in her chest, and as she awoke fully, the smell was so strong that she gagged. It was slightly different now, a rotten, decaying, almost sweet smell, full of noxious gases.

'Oh God, Oh God.'

The smell thickened, became a vapour, one that

she could see ballooning up from the floor, faintly yellow-green.

They did not sleep again but huddled together, cold and afraid, and in the end they dozed, and slowly became aware that the smell had faded and the vapour thinned away to nothing.

The children had not stirred.

There was no sound from the front room when Belinda went down. There was none at nine 'o' clock, then ten. Laurie pottered across the hall while she filled the dishwasher.

'Oh look,' she heard him say. 'Oh look.'

Solange was lying on top of the bed covers, fully dressed, her flesh mushroom-coloured, eyes wide open and sightless.

Two

'You are not to blame,' Pastor Lewis said several times, after the small, bleak funeral, which was not held in the chapel. Belinda had insisted they go straight to the crematorium. There was something purifying about a fire. She wanted to see it. If she had been brave, she might have asked to go behind the curtain, have them open the metal door and look into the heart of the furnace.

That night she slept better than she had since Solange had taken over the front room. The children's faces were smoothed of anxiety, their bodies seemed lighter, they skipped about. They ate and ate.

'What are we going to do with it?' Norman said.

'Leave it. Lock the door. I am never going in there again.'

'Don't be silly, Belinda.'

'You do what you like.'

'Well … let it all settle shall we?'

'Every morning I woke feeling as if cobwebs clung to my face. Every time I came home … opened the door … I could smell it.'

'I never really understood,' Norman said, 'about the smell.'

'Then there was something wrong with you.'

But he shook his head. Perhaps now she had gone, things really could go back to where they were, settled, Belinda happy in her routine, the children aware, without being able to express as much, that it was over.

'Why did she come here?' Fern asked once.

'She was very lonely. She was our relation and we wanted to do her a kindness. We thought it was for the best.'

Fern's small face tightened. For a second, she looked semi-transparent, as if her skin was the white of egg painted over her bones. Wallace never spoke of it. Laurie banged on the front room door occasionally but, getting no reply, wandered away. Soon, he stopped doing it altogether.

The year turned. The street smelled of burning leaves.

*

At the end of October, when the clocks had gone back and it was dark by five, Belinda came home to see a light in the front room – not a bright light, but as if someone had left a side lamp switched on. Perhaps Norman had gone into the front room the previous evening and left it on. But would one of them not have noticed?

She hesitated in the hall, outside the front room. She put her hand on the knob, then whipped it away. The knob felt red-hot. Touching it, it was as if her palm had been branded.

But when she looked at it in the kitchen, nothing showed, skin and flesh were normal. She said nothing to Norman when he came in except, 'Will you switch off the lamp in the front room?'

He pulled off his coat. 'You've been in there?'

'No, you must have left it on when you went in last night.'

They looked at one another. She knew what he was going to say and she would not let him say it.

'Just switch it off. No point in wasting electricity.'

He went into the hall and hung up his coat. She heard him go into the front room.

'There isn't a lamp on,' he said, 'You must have

made a mistake – it was probably the street light, reflecting on the glass.'

'Oh. Reflecting on the glass. Yes, of course.'

At supper, Wallace pushed his food around his
plate but ate nothing. The next morning he had
dark circles beneath his eyes. He did not touch his
breakfast.

'Let him stay off. It's Friday, he's probably devel-
oping a cold. Today at home and then the weekend
will see it off.'

The boy lay on the kitchen couch, covered in a
blanket. 'Is Solange coming back here forever?'

Belinda was writing up lesson notes at the table.
Outside the sky was sulphurous. A wind had got up.

'What do you mean? She isn't coming back here
at all. She died, Wallace.'

His small face was peaky pale, eyes large and
anxious. 'She was here in the night.'

'Of course she wasn't.'

'I knew you wouldn't believe me,' Wallace said,
but then squeezed his eyes tightly shut and would
not answer any of her questions.

Several times that night, while a storm broke
overhead and his room was vivid with blue-white
lightning, Wallace woke crying out with fear and

pushing something away from him with raised arms.

'She did go into his room that time,' Norman said. 'He's remembering that, dreaming about it. These things take a while to fade.'

After Wallace, Fern refused to eat, though she apparently had no nightmares and did not appear ill at first. But then she began to lose weight, so rapidly that her bones gleamed beneath the skin.

'Bit of a mystery.' The GP rolled down his sleeves. 'She's perfectly sound, everything as it should be, heart, lungs, all that, but I'll run a couple of tests, cover all bases.'

It was the same with Wallace. All tests were normal.

'A week in the sun – Madeira, Tenerife, that sort of thing?' Though he sounded doubtful. But neither of them could take the time out. Only Laurie continued hungry and cheerful.

Wallace woke two or three times every night screaming, and begged not to be left, so that in the end they put a mattress for him on their own bedroom floor. Fern never woke, but had become skeletal. And then the smell came back, filtering rankly into every room, together with a thin pus-coloured smoke that slipped through cracks in the door frames. They choked on it.

'I can't live here, I can't stand it any longer and isn't that exactly what she wants? So let her have it, let her win.'

'She?'

'You know, you've always known, for God's sake.'

'I don't understand any of it,' Norman said. His face looked grey, the whites of his eyes jaundiced.

'We don't have to understand, we just have to go.'

'But why would she want to hurt us? If you're implying that she is haunting us, why? Besides, it isn't possible.'

The following week he had to travel to a conference in Newcastle, staying away for two nights. The thought of being alone in the house paralysed Belinda with such fear that she could not swallow her food.

At nine on the first evening, she telephoned but got a voicemail.

'Please will you come round – or anyway, ring me back? Terrible things are happening here, we are being … we are …'

As she put down the receiver, she heard the door

of the front room open and close. She ought to go upstairs to the children but dared not even cross the hall. Footsteps, accompanied by the tap of two sticks, went instead, slowly along, tap-tap, slowly up, bump, bump. If it had not been for the thought of the children she would have lost all courage and cowered alone in the kitchen, but the woman, or the ghost of the woman, whoever was menacing this house and this family, was on her way to them.

Belinda flung open the kitchen door.

'Get down the stairs, get down, get away from here. What are you trying to do? What do you want from us? What did we ever do but give you a home? Why do you hate us? Why do you want to harm my children?'

The silence was absolute, as if felt had been stuffed and pressed deep in her ears.

'What do you *want?*'

The silence thickened. Her limbs, which had seemed immoveable, freed themselves and she flew up the stairs. No one stood in her way. The terrible silence was here too.

She had left the door of her bedroom ajar. The two older children were sleeping there, curled to face one another on their separate small mattresses. They were pale, and stick-thin.

As she backed out of the room, Belinda saw the shadow on the opposite wall. She stopped dead. The shadow shifted very slightly.

'Get away from here, leave us alone.' Her voice came out as a strange hiss.

The shadow stirred again, like a tree in the wind, but did not go. The silence was like the silence of deep snow. She could not hear the children breathing. Slowly, the shadow broke up, like a reflection in water hit by a stone, then dissolved and faded, until the wall was blank again.

There had been a faint trace of the old smell but that too had evaporated. She felt calmer, sure that for now, all was well again. Nothing troubled the house. The silence had become simply quietness, through which normal sounds filtered – a car in the street, the water pipes, the boiler firing in the kitchen, Wallace clearing his throat.

It was the noise of the doorbell shrilling that startled her, so that she leapt in fright. She went back to the children but they had not stirred. The bell rang again, for longer.

'Who is it?' She did not remove the door chain.

'Pastor Lewis. I got your message …'

Bitterly cold air streamed in when she opened the door, as if there was a frost.

179

'Whatever is it? You look shocked out of your wits Belinda, come into the warm.' The familiar kitchen, humming quietly, restored her.

'I'll make us a drink. Do you prefer tea, Pastor, I can't remember …?'

'You sit down, I'll make us tea. I'm sure I can find everything.'

She was glad to sit.

'Now tell me what this is about while I do the tea.'

He listened, said nothing, only let the story come out, in broken phrases at first and then in a stream, everything – it astonished her how much she re-membered, detail after detail.

He set down the pot and cups.

'Drink it hot and sweet.'

'I don't usually take …'

'This is not a usual situation.'

Everything that had swirled round her mind, like fragments in a shaken kaleidoscope, began to settle. A picture formed.

'It sounds like madness.'

'No, no.'

'Pastor Lewis, you talked to Solange, you seemed to get on quite well.'

'I was on my guard, all the same.'

'What do you mean?'

'I'm not easily taken in but of course I wanted things to resolve themselves. I wanted her to see some reason.'

'But she didn't, did she?'

'It would appear not.'

'When she died, I felt as if we had come out into the sunshine after living under a great blackness. I felt light as a feather.'

'I believe in evil, Belinda ... or why would the Lord's prayer have us ask to be delivered from it? We must believe in it.'

'Oh I do. She is evil, more so now than when she was alive. There is a pure evil now, isn't there, she need hold nothing back.'

'Evil, and the powers of evil, yes. But perhaps not ghosts, Belinda.'

He lifted his cup of tea. And then the sounds came.

First, footsteps ran down the stairs and across the hall. The front door opened, letting in a wild gust of wind. The Pastor's cup smashed into the saucer, breaking it, sending scalding tea across the table. The front door slammed shut and for a moment the house was absolutely still and silent again, before the crying began from upstairs.

Fern was half awake, sitting up and making a

slight moaning sound, but she settled again easily. Wallace was asleep, buried half under the covers, his pale hair sticking out round his head. They both looked thin and still.

'They're fine, Belinda, whatever disturbed them – the wind most probably. They're not harmed. Your nerves are like bare wires.'

'Why is she doing this? How is she doing it? Look at them. They barely eat, they have no life in them. They go about like flickering candles.'

Pastor Lewis stood looking at the children gravely, his face working, as if he were struggling with something and torn apart.

'I am not of a church that will perform exorcism,' he said after a long time, 'but it may be that we should look into it, in this case.'

A great relief took hold of her.

'Now you kiss your little ones and tuck them in. It will be morning before you know it.'

She was more grateful to him than she could express, thanking him again and again as she went from the elder two into Laurie's room.

Her scream stopped Pastor Lewis dead and froze his limbs, froze his nerves and the marrow in his bones. Laurie's bed was empty.

They raced round the whole house, calling out, but the house did not contain him.

Clever, cunning, Solange had taken the one thing she wanted but which she had, until the last moment, pretended to ignore.

He was never found, nor was any speck of physical evidence, no foot- or finger-print, not the least trace of any human being, other than those of the living family. Pastor Lewis struggled on at the chapel for some weeks before breaking down in both body and mind, and, for all anyone knew, in spirit.

Norman and Belinda moved, though not far away, to a bland box of a house, which was quite new and so held no past or memories. Not that the absence eased them or applied any balm to their hearts.

But Wallace and Fern began to eat again and to grow, to have colour in their cheeks and flesh on their bones. Solange had done with them, playthings and decoys as they had been.

PRINTER'S
DEVIL COURT

Inner Temple Library

Temple, Farley and Freeman. Solicitors
2 Delvers Court
St James's SW1

Dear Sir

The enclosed item has been sent on to me by Messrs.
Geo Rickwell, Antiquarian Bookseller, with the in-
struction that it be passed on to the beneficiaries of the
estate of the late Dr Hugh Meredith. As you know, the
library in which it was found was entrusted for sale to
Messrs Rickwell. Of a few items not included in the
sale, mainly for reasons of poor physical condition, the
enclosed was deemed to have no commercial value. I
am therefore sending it to you to deal with in any way
you see fit. I would be grateful for acknowledgement
of its receipt in due course,

Yours etc.

The book in question measures some eight inches
square and the sheets, of a pleasing cream paper, had
been folded and hand-sewn together with heavy card

backing – a neat and careful piece of amateur book-binding. Apparently this, together with botanical il-lustration and embroidery, was one of the soothing hobbies taken up by Dr Meredith in old age, when he had long ceased to practice medicine, not only because of his advancing years, the family story has it, but because he suffered from a sort of intermittent nervous condition.

The book has no title on the cover or the spine but on the first page is written:

The Wrong Life.

Hugh Meredith MD

The Book

In my first year as a junior doctor I moved into lodgings in a small court close by Fleet Street, an area which could not at the time have changed greatly since the days of Dickens. The court was small and the tall, narrow, grimy houses faced into a dismal yard, at one end of which a passageway led into the main thoroughfare. At the other end, a similar snicket led to the graveyard and thence to the church of St Luke-by-the-Gate. The church was pressed in on either side by two warehouse buildings and most of the graveyard was ancient and no longer in use. Old stones leaned this way and that, monuments and tombs were greened and yellowed over with moss and lichen. One or two trees struggled upwards to find what little light they could, and at their bases, more gravestones, sunken flat to the earth, were almost entirely obscured by weeds, ivy and rank grasses. In between was a mulch of dead leaves. I sometimes took a short cut through the churchyard on my way – often late – to the hospital. Once, when my sister was visiting me and I took her that way, she said that she could not understand why I was not frightened out of my wits when walking.

'Frightened of what?'

'Ghosts ... the dead.'

'As to ghosts, my dear Clara, I do not believe in them for a moment and dead bodies I see in the hospital every day so why would either of those things frighten me? The only thing to be wary of in these dark hidden corners of London are living thieves and pickpockets. Even the vagrants can be threatening after they have been drinking illicit cider.' I laughed, as nevertheless, Clara pulled me by the arm to hasten our way to the main gate.

When this story begins it's late and dismal autumn. Every morning mist rose and hung over the river after a cold night and when it turned milder for a day or two, the choking fog rolled over the city, muffling sounds, blurring the outlines of buildings and tasting foul in the mouth and nostrils, so that everyone went about with their faces half-covered in mufflers. Braziers burned at the street corners, where the hot chestnut and potato sellers rubbed hands stiff and blue with cold. Traffic crawled along the Strand to Fleet Street, headlamps looming like great hazy moons out of the mist. Fleet Street was a din of hot metal presses turning out the daily and evening newspapers. Open a small wooden door in a wall and you saw down into a bedlam of huge iron machines and the clatter of chutes, down which rolled the *Evening News* and *Standard*, *The Times* and the *Chronicle*, by the mile. Men at work below were dwarfed by the presses, faces grimy with oil and the air was thick with the smell of it and of fresh ink and hot paper. I loved it and wandered these old streets whenever I had a half hour to spare, venturing up unfamiliar passages and alleys into Courts and Buildings, discovering hidden churches and little gardens. But best of all I liked to walk beside the river, or to stand on the terrace of the medical school which overlooked its great flowing expanse, now treacle black, now sparkling in the sun and carrying so many and various craft on its tide. Such idle moments were rare, however. I was usually attending patients, following great physicians on their ward rounds, learning from the surgeons in theatre and the pathologists in the mortuary. I loved my work as I had loved every moment of my studies. I suppose the latest in a line of doctors would either take to medicine as a duck to water or rebel and become a bank manager.

Three other doctors lived at number two, Printer's Devil Court, at the time of which I write. Walter Powell, a year ahead of the rest, James Kent and Rafe McAllister. James and I occupied one floor, Walter and Rafe the other. It was a dark house, with steep, narrow stairs and we each had a miserably small bedroom and shared bathroom, with temperamental plumbing. But we had one large sitting room which stretched the width of the house and had a coal fire with a chimney that drew well, a reasonably comfortable sofa and three armchairs. There was a handsome mahogany table at which we ate and sometimes worked. The room had two windows, one at either end, in each of which stood a desk. There was precious little natural light and the outlook was of the opposite buildings. By now it was dark at four o'clock and lamps and fire were lit early. We kept irregular hours, sometimes working all day and all night, so that we only met to eat or relax together a couple of times a week. The landlady, Mrs Ratchet, rarely spoke a word but she looked after us well enough in her way, cleaning and clearing, making the beds and the fire and providing food at odd hours. We were fortunate, hard-working and innocent – or so I thought. I got on well with my fellows. James was a simple, easy-going man, with little imagination but a great deal of human sensibility. He was a plain-speaking and compassionate doctor in the making. Rafe was serious, studious and silent. He was never unfriendly and yet I could not get to know him – he presented a closed-off front and seemed to live in a world of test tubes and apparently dreamed only of finding cures for rare and obscure conditions. He had little to do with patients, which was probably for the best but I judged that one day he would make some remarkable medical breakthrough, in his own, intense and purposeful way.

Walter Powell was an even more complex character. If ever I felt a dislike or approval of any of my fellows, it was of him. He was jovial and friendly enough but he had a sly way with him and something shadowy in his personality though I could not have put a finger on quite what – at least not then. The only way I can give any idea of how he – and indeed, Rafe – affected me is to say that I would happily have entrusted my life to James but to Walter and Rafe, never.

Part Two

One

It was a murky November evening with a fog off the river and a fuzzy halo round every street lamp, when the conversation, which had such a hideous outcome, took place. We had all four of us returned to our lodging house earlier than usual and eaten our lamb stew and treacle pudding together at the big table – Mrs Ratchet knew how to line the stomachs of hungry young doctors in such bleak weather. Everything had been cleared away and we sat with the precious bottle of port, generously provided by James's wine merchant brother, around a good fire. James and Walter had lit their pipes and the sweet smell of Old Holborn tobacco was pleasing to the two of us who did not smoke.

We had begun to talk in an idle way about the day's work. I had been following an eminent thoracic specialist on his ward round, taking in as much as I could – he kept up a brisk pace – about rare lung diseases, and then working in the crowded outpatient clinics. Walter had been in the mortuary, assisting at the post mortems of bodies washed up or pulled out of the River Thames. One had been trapped under the hull of an abandoned barge for several weeks, he told us with a certain relish. I shuddered but he merely smiled his tight little smile.

'You will have to acquire a stronger stomach for the game, Hugh.'

'Hardly a game.'

He shrugged and for a moment we all fell silent. The fire shifted down. James bent forward and threw on another couple of coals. And then Walter said, 'What opinions do we all have about the story of the raising of Lazarus?'

I suppose the leap from bodies drowned in the River Thames to the New Testament story of the man miraculously raised from the dead by Jesus, was not such a great one but the question silenced us again.

'I'm not sure I remember many of the details,' I said at last. 'I rather switched off the chapel sermons in my senior school years.'

James said that he knew the story. Rafe did not speak.

'Or that of the centurion's daughter?' Walter

continued, taking the pipe from his mouth to smile again. I remember noticing what a pale complexion he had, even in the ruddy glow from the fire, which gave the others a more cheerful aspect. Walter's hair was already receding, showing his high forehead and oddly large skull.

'Come, you must all have some theory.'

'I am no biblical scholar,' James said, 'but for what it is worth, I believe fully in the stories. They have the ring of truth.'

'Of course,' Walter nodded. 'You, as a conscientious Christian would. But as a medical man?'

Rafe got up abruptly and went out. We heard his footsteps going up the stairs two at a time. He returned to the room carrying a Bible.

'Let us read the exact accounts before we express any further opinions.'

I noted that it took him almost no time to find the relevant pages, which surprised me as I had not put Rafe down as a religious man. We settled quietly while he read first, in two of the Gospels, the account of the raising of Jairus's daughter.

'Well, that seems quite straightforward,' James said. 'One line is conclusive and repeated in each gospel account. "The maid is not dead but sleepeth." As Jesus saw.'

'Yes, plenty of that sort of thing,' I said, 'we have all seen it – the deep coma resembling death. People have been pronounced dead and taken to the mortuary or even to the undertaker and consigned to their coffin, only to have woken again.'

'Perhaps that would take care of Luke, Chapter 7?'

Walter took up the Bible and, like Rafe, found the page almost immediately.

'When he came to the gate of the city, behold, there was a dead man carried out … And Jesus came and touched the bier and said "Young man, I say to thee, arise. And he that was dead sat up and began to speak."'

'More problematic all the same. The man was on the bier being taken for burial, which has to take place very quickly in hot countries,' Walter said. 'I vote that this was another case of the deep coma – the man had a lucky escape.'

James looked perturbed. Walter flipped the pages and found the story of the raising of Lazarus. 'Here,' he said, a slight smugness in his tone, 'this is unequivocal, I think.'

'Now he had been in the grave for four days …'

'Can we be sure of that ?' I asked.

'No, but the story is quite detailed – why would

they lie? His sister says, "by this time he stinketh for he hath been dead four days."'

Rafe looked blank yet I thought I caught the glint of something like excitement in his eyes.

'Listen then,' Walter continued, 'Jesus cried with a loud voice, "Lazarus, come forth." And he that was dead came forth, bound hand and foot with grave cloths and his face was bound about with a napkin.'

James sat back. 'And that,' he said, 'I do believe.'

Thinking to lighten the atmosphere, I knelt on the hearth rug and made up the fire, poking at it to loosen the ashes below, then adding more coals. The whole flared up so quickly that I started back and as I did so, I glanced round the room. James sat very still, his demeanour very calm. Rafe's face was closed and expressionless, his eyes down. Walter was looking directly at me with an expression I could not wholly read, but which seemed almost rapacious, so that I felt distinctly uncomfortable.

'I vote for another glass of port,' I said, 'if James would allow.'

He jumped up at once and busied himself over re-filling the glasses. When he had seated himself again, Walter said, 'You two were not here when Rafe and I began discussions on this subject.'

'Discussion about the miracles of Jesus Christ?' I said, surprised.

'Not exactly,' Walter leaned forward and I caught the same glint in his eyes as I had noticed in Rafe's.

'Oh, it was nothing but some macabre joking,' he said now, giving Walter a quick look, as if in warning. 'We had both had some encounters with death in its various forms that day and you know as well as I that we need a touch of gallows humour to see us through. That is why medical students tradi-tionally play such ghoulish tricks on one another.'

James laughed. 'Like Anderson in the dissecting room and ...'

Walter held out his hand. 'Yes, yes.' Something in his tone doused our mirth of the incident. 'But other than in those remote biblical times – and who knows how reliable the witnesses were after all? – Have any of us heard of men – or women, for that matter – being raised from the dead? By dead I mean exactly that. Dead.'

'Well of course not,' James said.

'Yet you are ready to believe in incidents recorded more than two thousand years ago.'

James nodded but said nothing.

'Let's leave biblical times. Do any of us believe

that this miracle could be performed now? Though clearly not by the man Jesus.'

'So what are you talking about?' I asked. 'Do you mean by those who serve in His ministry now?'

'No. By men like us – doctors and scientists that we are.' I saw that he and Walter exchanged another glance.

'Is this some fantasy you have been beguiling yourselves with on your walks to and from the hospital?' I asked, for Walter and Rafe generally went together. Now, Rafe leaned forwards with some eagerness.

'It is far more than that, and we are not men to waste time on fantasies.'

James looked troubled but I simply laughed.

'Enough teasing,' I said, 'you had better tell us, as it's the time of a dismal evening for a good tale.' My voice sounded over-loud and hearty in the room.

'I assure you that I am deadly serious and so is Rafe. But if you cannot be, let us say no more on the subject.' Walter tamped and fidgeted away with his pipe.

'Come now,' I said, 'I will take you at your word. Let us hear what you have to say and we can make up our own minds.'

Walter continued to work away at the pipe, like an

actor confident that he has his audience and can keep them waiting. Eventually it was lit to his satisfaction and he drew on it a few times before beginning.

'As you may have guessed by now, I have been considering our subject for some time. And because I am no more than a basic scientist, whereas Rafe here is a scientific genius, I have discussed it all with him. I have put difficult questions to him and he to me and we have each played devil's advocate. Now we have reached the point where we think we should bring you two into the secret. On one condition.'

He took the pipe from his mouth again and paused, enjoying the melodrama of the moment.

'So what is your condition, Walter?'

'That you must want to know, and know everything. If you do not – perhaps I will say "dare not" – we will continue to share these agreeable lodgings with you both as usual and never mention the matter again.'

Walter looked steadfastly at me and then at James and I was so mesmerised by the look in his eyes as he stared that I could not glance away.

'That is all very well,' I said, 'but how on earth can I tell you I don't want to hear a word more when I don't know what it is all about?'

'But you do. You have been given more than a hint – quite enough on which to base a decision.'

'The subject being the miracles of raising the dead?'

'Not precisely. As I said, we are not biblical scholars and those times are long past. It was a convenient way of introducing the nature of the business, that is all.'

'Well for my part,' James said, 'I don't understand any of it.' He looked at me. 'I must say that my instincts tell me to remain in ignorance – even in innocence.'

I paused. I was still more or less convinced that the whole thing was an elaborate game on Walter's part. Rafe's chair was pulled back into the shadows so that his face was hidden, only his spectacles occasionally gleaming in the firelight. Now he said quietly, 'Just remember that what you know you can never unknow. If you are afraid ...'

'Of course not. What trick could you two cook up that would be so alarming?'

Rafe did not reply.

'Make your decision,' Walter said.

'Before I reply,' I said, 'tell us why it is so important to make us party to whatever game you propose to play.'

'Because you may find it more interesting and remarkable than you suppose. Because you will be entirely impartial witnesses. And because we may need your help. It would not be easy to find two other men we know so well and more importantly, whom we trust.'

'Is this enterprise dangerous?'

'To you? I am not sure. But I can see no reason why you would be at serious risk of harm.'

'Is it legal?'

'I have no idea. I suspect that the law has never been tested in the matter.'

Suddenly, my mind was made up. I slapped the arm of the chair. 'Then, dammit ...'

But Walter held up his hand. 'Just one more thing, though I suspect I know what you have decided. If you are with us, you must swear solemnly that you will tell no one – no one. Now or at any time. If you are ever questioned, which is improbable, you must deny all knowledge or involvement.' His expression was as serious as a man's could be.

'Then I swear it,' I said, and as I did so, I felt an odd nervous lurch in my belly. 'I swear it and I am with you.'

Walter did not reply but turned to look at James, who had gone horribly pale.

'I cannot swear,' he said. 'I am not with you, whatever this nonsense is about and so I would rather not hear more.'

He got up quickly and nodding us 'good night', he left the room. We heard his footsteps and his door close. It was disconcerting. I liked and trusted James and for a moment, I thought of changing my mind. I looked at Walter and as I did so, I felt a flicker of alarm. Something in his eyes gave out a warning and a threat.

'Another glass of port,' I said hastily. 'I'm sure James would not object.'

Walter frowned. 'No, we need clear heads.'

I let the port stand but I tried to keep my tone light as I asked, 'Now – what is this all about? What are you proposing?'

'We are proposing,' Walter replied, 'to bring the dead back to life.'

Two

I slept soundly that night perhaps because I still believed that Walter's proposed experiment was nothing more than a jape. At first, nothing else happened, though I caught James looking at me anxiously once or twice. But then there were some subtle changes to our household routine. Rafe had apparently discovered some time earlier that the house had a basement room – no more than a cellar – which was empty and unused, and he persuaded our landlady to let it to him for a pittance. I returned home early one day with a feverish cold, to find him unloading what looked like half the contents of a laboratory and lugging it down the area steps. He certainly did not speak and I was feeling too rotten to ask any questions or offer him help.

The next time I saw him he was coming up from

the basement, slipping a key into his pocket. He rarely joined us at supper now and when he did, he ate quickly and immediately made off downstairs. There were no more leisurely, companionable evenings when we four sat talking round the fire. Walter seemed to spend longer hours at the hospital, especially at night and when he was home, kept to his own room. Shortly afterwards, I forgot about the whole secret episode because my head cold descended onto my lungs and the subsequent bronchitis put me first to bed for a week and then sent me away from London's foul winter air to the home of my family in coastal Norfolk. There, I regained my health and strength, albeit slowly, until I could take walks along the seashore and across the marshes. Nothing could have been better calculated to restore me.

Christmas came and went and we saw in the New Year merrily. I was preparing to return to London when on 2 January I received a telegram from Walter.

Enterprise critical stage.
Urgent you return and witness.

After the fogs and damp of late autumn, London had come in for one of the worst winters for decades.

Snow had fallen thickly for several days and then frozen hard to the ground every night. Temperatures remained below freezing and twice plummeted to depths barely known since the Great Frost, when the Thames had frozen over.

The fire made little impression on the air of the sitting room and our windows were ferned and feathered over with ice, on the inside. The hospital, of course, was full to bursting point: vagrants and beggars died on the streets in shameful numbers and we were all working round the clock. I had hurried back as requested but for over two weeks Walter had no time to talk to me and Rafe was unable to work in his cellar laboratory, the cold was so intense. James I almost never saw and when I did, I felt that he had withdrawn from me as well as from the others and was wary of conversation.

On a night in early March, when at last the thermometer hovered just above freezing, Walter knocked on my door well after one o'clock in the morning. He was wearing his outdoor clothes and there was something almost akin to an electrical charge about him, so that I jumped up from my desk in alarm.

'What has happened?'

'Nothing yet. But it is time. Come – Rafe is waiting.'

'Where are we going?'

'To the hospital. But we must go stealthily and take great care.'

The pavements were treacherous and piles of dirty, frozen snow lay in the gutters. The half-moon was hazy, so that we had to watch our every step, and a raw and bitter wind blowing off the river scoured our faces.

The lamps at the hospital entrance gates glowed out but much of the building was dimmed, as people slept. We entered by the front doors and at once turned along a covered way to the old East Wing and then down three flights of stairs that led to the basement corridors. Walter's footsteps made barely a sound and I thought that he must have walked this way at night many times before. Once or twice he stopped, raised his hand, and listened, before continuing. I followed in his footsteps, barely able to breathe, I was so tense. We turned a corner into a short passageway with an unmarked double-door at the end. No one else was about. This part of the hospital was little used, though the old wards had been hastily re-commissioned to cope with the overflow of patients. The whole place smelled cold and slightly damp. We stopped and Walter tapped on the door, though not on the panel but on the frame, presumably so that the sound was muffled. At once, it was opened by Rafe. He so rarely gave anything away on his impassive features but now he wore an expression of scarcely concealed excitement and I felt the same strange electrical charge coming off him as I had noticed with Walter.

The second we were both inside, Rafe turned the key in the lock. The two did not speak as they moved into the centre of the small room. It was windowless, save for a row of rectangular panes high up along one side, and the walls were tiled to the ceiling. Two lamps stood on a laboratory bench, only one of which was lit and that dimly but it was enough for me to see about me.

Next to the lamps stood a small array of laboratory paraphernalia – test tubes, rubber piping, glass phials. A bunsen burner gave out a low, steady blue flame and there were a couple of items of medical equipment. In the body of the room stood a hospital trolley, levered to its full height and with the metal sides raised. On it was a still figure covered in a single grey blanket. I went closer, and saw that it was the body of an old man. His head was covered in grey stubble, with the same forming a close beard. His skin was bruise coloured and grime enseamed the neck, the skin below his eyes, and around the nose and ears. Clearly, though he looked to have been given a cursory wash, the dirt was ingrained so as to have become almost a part of the scheme itself. One hand was uncovered, the nails had recently been cut but more dirt was wedged beneath them and in the creases of the fingers.

At first glance, I took this to be a corpse but then I saw the faintest of movements as the breath rose and fell in the man's chest. Walter bent down and put a finger under the nostrils and nodded. The man's breathing was laboured and as we stood looking at him a rattle came from his throat. Walter glanced at Rafe and it was as if a flint had been struck and the quick spark passed between them.

'Yes,' Walter said, 'not long. A moment or two only but the old ones put up a brave fight. Life has been hard to them and they are used to battling.'

I started to say something but at first my voice refused to come out and I could only make a hoarse croaking sound, as if it was I and not the old man fighting for breath. But eventually, I managed to speak.

'Who is he?'

Walter shrugged. 'Brought in from the street a couple of nights ago, half frozen to death and full of pneumonia. He had nothing on him but his clothes.

His pockets were full of chestnut husks – he had probably been living off the scraps of nuts that fell onto the pavement and perhaps tossed a whole one now and again by the seller.'

'No name?'

'No name, no home, no family, no friends, no hope. He is not long for this world and will be better out of it.'

I had an uprush of terror as he said it, and took a quick step nearer to the trolley on which the old man lay.

'You are surely not thinking of hastening his end, for some foul purpose? The man is dying and will be at peace soon enough. I will not stand by and watch you commit murder.'

Walter put a hand on my arm. 'No, my friend, we are doctors in the business of saving life, not disposing of it.'

'You swear?'

'I swear.'

I turned to Rafe, who nodded.

'Then I have done you an injustice.'

'No matter. But I am puzzled as to why you should think either Rafe or myself likely to be common murderers.'

I did not know. I could not say that something

217

about their manner had been troubling me sorely and that this urgent journey to the bowels of the hospital at the dead of night had thoroughly unnerved me.

'Nevertheless, I think I am entitled to some explanation of all this.'

'You are and before long you will be our witness and I swear to you that we plan nothing nefarious and nothing to endanger a life which is about to draw up to a peaceful end.'

Walter stepped forward and put his hand out to the man who lay there, breathing with more and more difficulty. The rattle in his throat was more pronounced and once or twice, the grimy fingers and hand twitched. Once the eyelids seemed about to open but then did not. The gas in Rafe's burners hissed and popped softly, otherwise the room was quite silent.

Had Walter and Rafe succumbed to some sort of madness? But what sort would grip two men together yet not also cause them to appear feverish and raving? Insanity is not infectious unless it comes about as the result of some rabies-like infection and they both seemed eminently well.

They could simply have been two doctors paying close attention to a patient for whom all hope had gone. What was I doing there, I as sane as any other, for all that I felt nervous and baffled? Walter had said that I was their witness but what was I witnessing? Only an old man dying.

In the next moment something happened, his raucous breathing changed, slowed and quietened.

'Now!' Walter said in an urgent tone and at once, Rafe crossed to the bench and took up a glass phial, a length of narrow tubing and a test-tube, together with what resembled an oxygen mask, but with a couple of alterations. He went up to the dying man and put the mask over his face. It sat loosely and he appeared quite unaware of it – indeed, I thought that the man was unaware of everything now. One end of the tubing was fixed to the mask and the other into the top of the phial and secured by a clip. The phial had two small holes in the side. Rafe held the test tube up and I saw some clear liquid, perhaps to a depth of half an inch, in the bottom. We were now all standing in such silence and stillness that our own breathing seemed to slow almost to a stop. There was no sound.

The old man's face was sunken in, the flesh already waxen. He breathed two more shallow breaths, then a third. I thought that I could hear the pounding not only of my own heart but that of Walter and Rafe's, too.

There came one more, unsteady breath and Walter said again 'Now!' But in a voice so faint that I barely heard him. On the same instant, Rafe poured the clear liquid out of the test tube into the phial. The old man exhaled for the last time and the breath travelled down from the mask over his face into the tubing. For a split second I saw it mist the inside of the glass. He breathed no more and at the very second that he was still, and in death, the liquid in the phial seemed to catch fire and to turn not into an ordinary flame but a sort of phosphorescent gas that crept up the inside of the glass, a very slightly pulsating substance, semi-transparent and astonishingly beautiful. I gazed at it in amazement and in disbelief. It remained when Rafe disconnected the tubing and quickly stopped the aperture. He held up the phial. I glanced at Walter and saw that he was transfixed by it and that his face wore an almost beatific expression – partly of triumph and partly what I can only call joy. Then he gave a small sigh and we all looked at the old man. His chest did not rise. He was utterly still and his face was changed by a look of utter tranquillity. Walter bent and lifted each of his eyelids and then beckoned me to move closer. He handed me his ophthalmic torch and I bent to examine the corpse's pupils.

'Fixed and dilated,' I said.

'Pulse?'

I held first one wrist then the other, for a full minute and put my finger to the carotid artery. I took the stethoscope and listened closely to the chest. There was nothing – no breath, no heartbeat, no sign of life at all.

'To the best of my knowledge and observation, this man is dead.'

There was an almost reverential hush. Rafe stood on the other side of the trolley, holding the glass. The beautiful light contained within it gleamed silver white and still phosphorescent and as we stared at it we saw that it still pulsed faintly in time with the beating of our hearts.

'So – there we have it,' Walter said.

I managed to pull myself out of my half-trance.

'I suppose you call whatever is in that phial "the spark of life" and I presume you now have plans to replace it into the dead body and wait for a resurrection?' I shuddered. The room was deathly cold, though I had been quite unconscious of the fact until now. I was badly frightened and completely out of my depth medically, ethically and simply as a human being. Walter touched my arm and I jumped back. His eyes were still sparking with excitement but his voice was full of concern.

'No,' he said. 'This man, whoever he is, will now be left to rest in peace and accorded a proper burial, by the Christian church – for which, by the way, though not a member, I have a profound respect.'

'Close by,' Rafe said, still holding the phial, which continued to gleam and pulsate, 'is the hospital mortuary, to which our friend here will now be taken. And then we plan to conduct the next and most vital phase of our experiment. I am warning you now, as I have warned Walter many times, it is the part most is likely to fail, though I have a flicker of confidence, based on experiments I have already conducted in my laboratory.'

'The cat!'

'Indeed, but after all, one ginger cat may easily be confused with another and besides, the cat is a living organism but it is not a human being. It lacks many attributes of the human and many religious people would say that a cat has no soul.'

I felt giddy and put my hand to my head. 'Is this night never to end? Will there be no conclusion to the strange events?'

As I swayed, Walter took firm hold of me and held me, while letting me slide gently to the floor. He propped me up with my back against the wall and then pushed me forwards with my head between my knees.

'If you still feel unsteady in five minutes, I will take you home. You are a robust man but you were gravely ill at the end of last year and you have just been subjected to a severe nervous strain.'

'No,' I said, as the swirling sensation behind my eyes gradually slowed, like a fairground carousel coming to a standstill. 'No, I intend to see this through. I am your witness and I won't let you down.'

'Good man. Now drink this.' He held a small flask. 'No no, it is simply a good brandy, it will do you nothing but good. I intend to have a dram myself.'

I took a good mouthful and the liquid fire of it re-invigorated me in seconds. I stood up. Walter was ready with a hand but I did not need it.

'I am quite well,' I said, 'and quite ready.'

Three

We covered the face and body of the old vagrant with a sheet and Walter and Rafe left the small room, Rafe pushing the trolley, Walter walking a step or two ahead. The corridors were empty and silent – any sounds from the main body of the hospital did not penetrate this subterranean annex. The old mortuary – there was a much newer one in the East Wing – was close by and unattended because it was now little used, but because of the recent influx of mortally ill patients, it was fully equipped and functioning. Walter had a key – I did not ask how he had obtained it.

'Is Rafe not coming with us?'

'We have things to attend to in readiness. You will stay here and guard our departed friend.' He glanced almost fondly at the sheeted body.

'Where are you going?'

'You seem nervous – surely you are accustomed to death by now?'

'I am agitated about what you and Rafe are doing. You must agree that it is hardly regular or normal.'

'It is unique,' Walter said.

'Perhaps, but as to remaining alone here with our friend – of course I am not nervous.'

'I am pleased to hear it,' Walter smiled and I realised what had always perturbed me about that smile. It was not sinister, though it was not especially pleasant but it had an odd effect. It changed his face from that of a young, fresh-faced man into one far older. It was uncanny. He was twenty-six but instantly became ancient, his features showing briefly the ravages of old age and bitter, even terrible experience. He glanced at me as he closed the mortuary door, leaving me alone and as the smile had faded his face was young again, the face on which few cares or troubles had made any mark. How peculiar, that the change should be wrought by a smile.

Being alone with a dead man did not perturb me in the least and I lifted the sheet to look again at his face. It still wore the expression of great calm and acceptance. I could discern, beneath the ravages of a hard lived life, and of ageing, that the man had once been handsome, with a broad brow and a well-shaped and resolute mouth. There was a gentleness about him which was delightful and strangely comforting. Whatever his life had been, death had resolved all suffering and troubles. I covered his face. No, I was not in the least afraid of a corpse which could do me no harm, but I was terrified of what living men might be about. The phrase 'playing with fire' came to mind, followed by remembrance of horrible stories, so that I was relieved when I heard the key being turned in the lock.

Rafe came in first, still carrying the glass phial, as if it contained a rare and precious oil. Walter was at his heels, pulling another trolley into the room, upon which another figure lay. He locked the door behind him.

'What —?'

He did not answer but stationed the trolley under the lamp.

'I need to call upon you again,' he said to me. 'You are my witness.'

He drew down the sheet and I caught my breath. The body was that of a young woman of eighteen or twenty years, wearing a green cotton hospital gown. Her hair was a rich brown, with the reddish tinge of a chestnut fresh from its carapace. Her skin was flawless. She was beautiful.

'Again,' Walter said at my side, 'as with our other body, we do not know her identity. She was brought into the hospital two days ago, found gravely ill with hypothermia on the river embankment. I attended to her and saw at once that here was the other half of the equation – if that does not put it too crudely. We made strenuous efforts to save her but when it became clear that we would not do so, I called Rafe. When I arrived here with you earlier, I hastened to find our old man and ascertain how much longer he had to live.'

All three of us looked down at the young woman. She was still breathing in a shallow and faltering rhythm. Walter felt her pulse.

'Weak and very slow.' His voice dropped to a whisper so that I felt he was talking to himself. 'If only she knew. If only …'

'I hope you do not intend to do her any injury or harm. Leave her to slip away peacefully, for God's sake. Leave your shabby experiments at least to the old and hopeless.'

Walter simply shook his head and did not reply. All gazed silently at the dying girl. There was no harsh rattle this time, merely a few sounds in her throat, as if she was trying to cough. Walter turned urgently to Rafe, who held the phial containing the pulsating phosphorescence, and a fresh oxygen mask which he quickly attached to the girl's face.

'Careful – wait – be very careful,' Walter said urgently. My mouth was dry, my eyes staring so that I scarcely blinked.

On the instant and without further warning, the girl's breathing stopped and at once the shadow of death, invisible yet almost tangible, crept over her face.

'Now!'

A split second and Rafe had started to squeeze the tube attached by one end to the phial and the other to the girl's mouth beneath the mask. The liquid flared up and became radiant as it travelled at great speed out of the phial until the glass was empty. We all held our breath and then I felt as if the air in the whole room had somehow lightened and taken on a life of its own. I felt my heart leap, I felt jubilant, joyous, more alive than I had ever been. I felt new-born. When I looked at the others, I saw by a strange pearlescence on their skin and light in their eyes that they experienced it too. It all lasted only a thousandth of a second and yet it seemed to last for all eternity, and when it faded, I felt as if I had been let down from the air, to land softly, safely, on the ground by Rafe's side. I did not dare to think, speculate, hope. I let my mind go blank. My body seemed held together by the finest of wires, which was taut but quite painless. And then I looked down.

The girl was breathing. Her pallor had the faintest colouring as the blood re-filled arteries, veins, capillaries, just below the skin. Her fingernails were flushed pink. She did not open her eyes, her body did not stir. Walter passed me the stethoscope and I could feel the trembling in his hand. I bent over the now living girl and listened to her heartbeat, heard the sound of air passing in and out of her lungs. I felt her pulse and lifted each eyelid in turn. The pupils were bright but unseeing. She was not conscious but as I removed the stethoscope, I said, 'I have no doubt that she is alive.'

Walter grabbed Rafe's hand in a grip so tight that the man winced.

'You have succeeded!'

Rafe was deathly pale.

'You have raised the dead!'

'No!' I said, and was startled to hear how loud and emphatic my voice sounded in the quiet room. 'You go too far. Your claim is too immense – it is not credible. It defies everything I know, or I have been taught – it defies human experience.'

'Yes,' Walter said, 'it does indeed. But now we

must be practical. The young woman must be taken back to an acute ward and put under close observation. I will take her myself and instruct the nursing staff. Rafe must attend to the dead man. We will meet again at Printer's Devil Court where my prescription is a glass each of good brandy.'

We watched Walter wheel away the still-breathing young woman. Our own work was quickly done. We left the old mortuary and locked the door. Rafe took possession of the key and we went, neither of us speaking, out of the hospital and up through the dark and deserted streets in the bitter cold, to our lodgings.

Four

'One thing I do not understand and that is why?
What possible reason could you have for perform-
ing this whole charade?'

We were all three of us sitting round the fire,
which was smoking and sulking dismally in the
grate, in spite of our best efforts. None of us was
calm enough to sleep. I had said nothing on the way
home or for some time after we had all our brandy
and battled with the fire but I had been thinking hard,
my brain trying to produce a plausible explanation
for what had happened, which had shocked and unnerved me until, as if some piece finally clicked into
place, I saw what should have been clear all along.
Walter and Rafe had performed an elaborately
staged series of clever conjuring tricks.

'You went to a good deal of trouble,' I said now.

'You prepared the way carefully and prepared me too for that matter and at some considerable risk. I see it all but I still do not see a reason, so perhaps before we retire please, Walter and Rafe, an explanation.'

Then I saw that Walter was angry. His mouth was tight, his eyes narrowed.

'You do not understand – *you*? Correct me, Hugh, but I think *we* are the ones owed an explanation and an apology.'

'How so?'

'Do you not believe the evidence of your own eyes? How can what you witnessed tonight be some kind of trick or charade? If it had been, then I agree you would be fully entitled to ask for a reason and an explanation, but credit us with more intelligence and maturity. What possible reason indeed could be behind such a trick? What a puerile game we would have been playing, what a waste of our time and energy – what an offence that would have been.'

'You cannot expect me to believe that it was anything other than a fraud.'

'I do expect it. What we witnessed was a triumphant success – the culmination of much work and strain over many months and many setbacks.'

I stood up. 'So you refuse to give me your reason – so be it. I am horrified that you should have played

such macabre games with the bodies of your patients. Shame on you. I want no more part of it. I
will find new lodgings. I bid you both good night
and God grant you forgiveness which is better than
you deserve.'

I did not go to bed, merely took off my jacket and
shoes, loosened my collar and sat in my chair for the
few hours that remained of the night, in a turmoil
of confused and angry thoughts. I could not forget
the sight of the old vagrant dying before us, and the
look of release and acceptance on his face. I could
not forget the sight of the beautiful young woman in
her coma, in that cold basement room. I intended to
scour the hospital on the following day, to find her
and discover what state she was in and whether she
was expected to recover. About Walter and Rafe I
could do nothing. I had, of course, no evidence of
their nefarious activities. I wanted nothing more to
do with them and prayed that whatever the reason for
their dark and secret games, they would now cease to
dabble in them and let the dead and the dying alone.

I wish now that I had taken James's course. I could
never *un*-know what I now knew or forget whatever
it was that I had witnessed. James would be deeply
troubled not the least because, in his eyes, they had

spoken blasphemously in their casual talk of 'raising the dead' and even gone on to pretend that they had done so. I might almost have believed them, had the old man, who I had confidently pronounced dead, woken. He had not. He had remained dead. The young woman, of course, had never been dead at all.

Altogether, I was ashamed to have had the smallest part in it.

I felt unwell the next morning, weak and exhausted. I did not go into the hospital and on the day after that, being worse, I again took myself to Norfolk, where I became seriously ill, my nervous system shattered, and I spent many weeks recuperating. I suffered from appalling nightmares and waking terrors, so much so that our family physician questioned whether I was fit to return to the hospital and continue my medical career. This roused me, and I realised how badly my body, mind and spirits had been affected. But that was my turning point. I pulled myself up, determined to return to the practice of medicine.

A year later I left London for a hospital in the West Country. I worked hard, my interest and enthusiasm fully roused again and gradually, I forgot Walter, Rafe and all their sinister trickeries.

James wrote to me to say that he had abandoned medicine, to study for the Ministry. Of Walter and Rafe, I heard nothing.

Part Three

Five

I travelled to London rarely. In the past twenty years, I had visited no more than half a dozen times. I had a horror of the place and I had never again ventured to my old hospital nor set foot near Fleet Street and its environs. Many people enjoy revisiting old haunts but a shadow fell on me if I so much as thought about them.

I practised as a country physician in a most beautiful and peaceful part of England for almost forty years and married a young widow, Eleanor Barnes, who brought me a fine brace of stepsons. We did not produce any children of our own but that had never troubled me. Both Eleanor's boys had grown up to be fine young men. Toby had gone into the army, Laurie had followed in my footsteps and I took a great deal of interest and pleasure in observing his progress through medical school and into his career as a doctor. He had no desire to be a family physician in a country parish – bury himself, as he put it, but went into medical research, made a pioneering study of certain genetic defects in children and became the country's leading expert in their diagnosis and treatment. He spent some time travelling abroad. Earlier in the year of which I now write, he had finally returned and came down to see us. He was in his late thirties by then, the prime of life, a tall, handsome man with his mother's deep brown eyes and sweetness of temperament.

We were only the three of us at dinner on that first night after his return and when the beef had been set on the table, Laurie said, 'That looks a fine bottle of claret you have opened, Hugh.' (He and Toby had never called me by anything other than my Christian name since childhood, in accordance with our wishes and out of respect for their late father.)

'Good enough for a toast.'

'It is indeed,' I said, touching the St Emilion from an especially fine year. 'Tell us what news you have that deserves toasting.'

Eleanor looked at her son, a slight flush coming to her cheeks. 'Are you going to be married, Laurie?'

He let out a shout of laughter. 'Whenever have

I had the chance to look around for a wife? No, no, you will have to wait a long time before that happens. I have been appointed as consultant physician at St Luke's – your own hospital, Hugh!'

In the midst of the general rejoicing and congratulations, a sudden chill descended on me, so that I had to force myself to remain full of laughter and good spirits, but it passed before long. I was proud of Laurie and delighted for him but I never wanted to set foot in that hospital again. However, some six months after he had taken up his appointment, I was obliged to do so.

Laurie was presenting a paper to a learned medical society, a great honour, and of course I must attend. Eleanor was away on a visit to her aged mother so that I went up to London alone. Laurie booked me a room in St Luke's club – for past and present members of the hospital. It was well-appointed, the public rooms were delightfully comfortable, in an old-fashioned way and I went off to hear the lecture wondering why I did not come to London more often, country bumpkin that I had become.

After the event, we enjoyed a celebratory dinner and then, as Laurie wanted to stay up into the small hours talking to his colleagues, I left them to it. Just before midnight I set off to walk back to the club.

My route was the old one, but this corner of London had changed a good deal. Fleet Street no longer housed the hot- metal presses and many of the old alleys and courts had long gone, most of them bombed to smithereens by the Blitz. Once or twice I took a wrong turn and ended up among new buildings I didn't recognise. At one point, I retraced my steps for a hundred yards and suddenly I was thrown back in time. I realised that the old Printer's Devil Court, where I had lodged, had been laid waste and that the hospital club was now sited on part of the same ground. I thought little of it – Printer's Devil Court held no special memories for me, other than those last peculiar and unpleasant ones.

I was about to turn into the club when I noticed that there was still a passageway to one side and saw the tower of St-Luke's-at-the-Gate rising up ahead of me in the fitful moonlight. I stood stock still. London churches are always a fine sight and I was glad that this one, with a surprising number of others, had escaped destruction. The passageway ended at the back of the old graveyard, as before, and that seemed unchanged, the tombstones still leaning this way and that and even more thickly covered in moss.

And then I saw her. She was a few yards away

from me, moving among the graves, pausing here and there to bend over and peer, as if trying to make out the inscriptions, before moving on again. She wore a garment of a pale silvery grey that seemed strangely gauze-like and her long hair was loose and free. She had her back to me. I was troubled to see a young woman wandering here at this time of night and started towards her, to offer to escort her away. She must have heard me because she turned and I was startled by her beauty, her pallor and even more, by the expression of distress on her face. She came towards me quickly, holding out her hand and seeming about to plead with me, but as she drew near, I noticed a curious blank and glassy look in her eyes and a coldness increased around me, more intense than that of the night alone. I waited. The nearer she came the greater the cold but I did not – why should I? – link it in any way to the young woman, but simply to the effects of standing still in this place where sunlight rarely penetrated and which had a dankness that came from the very stones and from the cold ground.

'Are you unwell?' I asked. 'You should not be here alone at this time of night – let me see you safely to your home.'

She appeared puzzled by my voice and her body trembled beneath the pale clothes.

'You will catch your death of cold.'

She stretched out both her hands to me then but I shrank back, unaccountably loathe to take them. Her eyes had the same staring and yet vacant look now that she was close to me. But she was fully alive and breathing and I had no reason to fear.

'Please tell me what is wrong?'

There was a second only during which we both stood facing one another silently in that bleak and deserted place and something seemed to happen to the passing of time, which was now frozen still, now hurtling backwards, now propelling us into the present again, but then on, and forwards, faster and faster, so that the ground appeared to shift beneath my feet, yet nothing moved and when the church clock struck, it was only half past midnight.

'Please help me. I need someone to help me.'

I would have replied again to ask her how I could help but I was silenced, not by her words, but by her voice, which was not that of a girl of no more than eighteen or twenty, but of an old man, a deep, hoarse voice, cracked and wavering. It was like hearing a puppet-master accidentally speaking in the voice of one doll while pulling the strings of another. I recoiled but I also went on staring at the girl not only because of the voice but because now I knew that I had seen her before – in the basement room of the hospital some forty years earlier, lying on a trolley and subject to the vile tricks played by Walter and Rafe.

'Sir? I have been searching for so long. Please help me.'

She was walking away from me and now began to move in and out between the graves again, going to first one and then another, quickening her pace, faster and faster, so that she seemed to be floating just above the ground. At each stone she bent and peered briefly at the inscription, though most of them were so overgrown and worn away by the weather, that few were legible. I followed her every step. I could not help myself. But at each grave, she let out a low, harsh cry of disappointment.

'Tell me,' I said, 'I will try to help you. Are you looking for a particular grave? That of a parent perhaps? A loved one? Let us look together, though we had really better do it in the daylight.'

She sank to the ground then and bent her head. 'My own ...' she said.

'Your own family? Or perhaps even your own child?'

She shook her head violently, as if she was angry that I did not understand.

'Taken ...' She seemed to have greater difficulty

in forming the words now, as if she had little breath left and her voice sounded even older.

'The … wrong … life …'

My blood felt as if it flowed more and more slowly through my veins and I felt the chill tighten around me again. I looked in horror at the young woman and as I did so, one moment she was there, kneeling on the cold ground trying desperately to speak, and the next, she seemed to be dissolving, to become absorbed, like the damp, into the rough earth in front of the grave. I closed my eyes in terror of what I was seeing and when I opened them again she had gone. She was simply no longer there before me. Nothing was there. Nothing at all.

Seconds later, I seemed to be dissolving too and then the stones around me and the walls of the church, all seemed to shimmer and fade and then go black.

I surfaced from a swirl of nightmares to find Laurie bending over me and as his features materialised from the mist, I realised that I was in my bed at the club. He told me that he and some fellows had taken a short cut home from their evening at the hospital dinner and found me lying insensible. Having checked that I was not injured but had merely fainted, they had carried me back between them.

I recovered quickly, my head cleared and after drinking some brandy and hot water, I sat beside the fire. It was then that I told the whole story to Laurie, from the events in my days at the hospital and Printer's Devil Court. When I reached the climax of the tale, with Rafe transferring the contents of the phial to the dead young woman, Laurie started up.

'Walter Powell! That name is known in the medical world – though I know you never hear a word of these things, buried as you are in the country. His name is known and so is that of his cohort, Rafe McAllister. They were apprehended in the course of stealing a body from the mortuary at St Luke's and from taking away a patient who was on the point of death, without permission or authority. A night porter gave testimony and one of his fellows swore to having seen the two men about their dreadful business more than once. He had alerted the hospital authorities but nothing was done. In fact, that porter was dismissed – I dare say he was believed to have had a breakdown. Nothing more was reported for over a year, when the two men were caught and police were called. I only know all this from hospital legend and reading up old newspapers. A macabre and distasteful business and quite inexplicable. I was mildly interested. I like to study peculiarities of human behaviour, as you know, but I came to the conclusion that it must all have been some money-making lark – that or blackmail though God knows how or what. The days of Burke and Hare are long gone.'

'Did you hear what happened to the two men? Presumably they went to jail.'

'I have no idea – I gave up reading about it – I'm far too busy. I know they were given bail on the usual conditions, that they surrender their passports and report to the police but more than that …' Laurie held out his hands.

'Meanwhile, Hugh, you are obviously sickening for something. Whatever caused you to pass out must be investigated – I am having you in St Luke's first thing tomorrow.'

It was clear that he had not taken my story seriously but put it down to the ravings of a man with a fever-ish illness of some kind. But I knew that the scene was no delusion. It was as real as the furniture in that club bedroom.

'I have no need of any hospitalisation, thank you Laurie. I am tired and a little chilled. A good night's sleep will sort that out and I will be right as rain to-morrow. I will return to my quiet, dull ways in the

depths of the country, where no ghost has ever troubled me.'

He knew that I meant what I said and got up to
leave, but at the door he turned.

'I do not believe in ghosts,' he said, 'nor in the
raising of the dead to life.'

'No. Until tonight, nor did I.'

He sighed and left, saying that he would check on
me in the morning before he would countenance my
going home.

As soon as he had gone, I felt restless and anxious,
not for myself but for the young woman, whatever –
whatever she was. She had asked me for help. Did she
linger about the churchyard night after night searching and pleading?

I dressed and went downstairs. The night porter's
cubby-hole had a low light showing within and the
man was leaning back in his leather armchair, eyes
closed, snoring gently, but as soon as I started to
creep towards the outer door, he woke.

'Are you well, sir? What can I do for you?'

'I need to take a turn in the air. Would you be so
kind as to let me out?' He looked perturbed.

'I should not be gone long but I find this is usually
the way to settle myself if I am restless.'

He unlocked a side door to the main entrance and

told me it would be open and he himself awake, on my return.

'Don't stay out too long, Sir, or hang about the back streets – you never know, at this hour.'

I knew that I would see her. She was wondering anxiously among the graves, just as before, leaning down to read the inscriptions. I made no sound but she turned, as if sensing my presence. Her expression was lost, distraught and she lifted her arm up.

'Help me. I cannot find … Find …'

The voice was old, as before, that of an old man. It was still so very strange and unnerving but I forced myself to remain calm.

'What are you looking for? You know that if I can help you I will.' She covered her eyes with her hands.

'Don't be afraid of me.' She said nothing.

'Tell me again.'

'I have … I am … Nothing.'

'What are you looking for?'

'I am … Not. I have … Not.' She gave a long and weary sigh and her whole body shuddered. 'The wrong life.' The words came out after a great effort. 'Help me … I must … Must … Find.'

What those two men had tried to do was not possible, and it was madness, terrifying and unimaginable, but that their terrible experiment had somehow succeeded in part I could not now doubt. The life force they had captured and transfused was no mere anonymous breath or spark, it was imprinted with the character – the being – the soul even – of the dead man. Was this young woman still alive or had she died a second time and this for good? Had she been unable to rest, or move on until she was rid of 'the wrong life' and re-united with her true self? Was she a ghost? But she spoke. Does a ghost speak? How could I know?

The next moment, again, she was no longer there. Had she slipped away, out of the side gate? Gone into the church perhaps? But I would have seen her, sensed some movement. She had not passed me. The moon was behind clouds, it was pitch dark but my eyes were so well adjusted to it that I could make out the graves, the wall, the church tower. I waited. I called out but my voice sounded oddly hollow and unreal, fading into the emptiness.

The next morning, I told Laurie I had changed my mind and wanted to stay another night. I needed to look up a few bits of information in the hospital records.

I found everything. The old man was listed as Patient A207. He had been certified dead by Walter Powell M.D. Touchingly, although I learned that the A stood for Anonymous, he had been given a burial name – John.

A young woman, Patient A194, was recorded a couple of days earlier, having been picked up from the street in an unconscious state. A locket had been found on her person with the name Grace barely visible on it. But there was no record of her death until several years later when again she had been found out of doors, suffering from malnutrition and hypothermia. The death certificate had been signed by a P. R. Ross M.D. but there was a pathologist's report inserted – a post-mortem had been requested by the coroner, as was by then becoming usual for those found dead on the streets of London. The body was that of a young woman aged around twenty-five to twenty-eight. She was severely malnourished, but this would not have accounted for her having the vocal cords, larynx and lungs of someone over seventy years of age, who had been a heavy tobacco smoker. 'Inconsistent with other findings' was jotted to one side in the usual pathologist's barely legible hand.

I closed the record book with a strange feeling of

relief. I had to find one further piece of information and then I would have all I needed to bring the whole business to a conclusion. If I was insane, hallucinating or suffering the effects of a brain injury, then I had no symptoms. I had a clear head, a calm mind, a steady pulse and a resolution as firm as I had ever known.

I did not mention any of it to Laurie. We ate supper together, during which he was full of medical talk. He glanced at me sharply once or twice, but I thought that everything about my demeanour and easy conversation put him at ease. When I told him that I was to travel home the next day on the late morning train I saw the relief in his eyes and I understood it fully. How could he possibly have believed my story? He was, like me, a doctor and a scientist and he knew far more than I did about delusional states. Although the boundaries of what was possible in medicine had been pushed farther than I would have ever thought possible as a young doctor, they surely could never extend to raising the dead. If what Walter and Rafe had done was real, we had better throw away all our textbooks and templates and prior assumptions, for the very ground on which we stood was unstable. Whatever the truth, whatever I had seen, I knew I must make a last attempt to lay it all to rest. If I did not, I feared I would never sleep again.

Just after one o'clock in cold clear moonlight I was waiting for her again, and again she seemed to materialise on an instant and was wandering among the graves as before. When she looked up and saw me, she beckoned. She wore the same thin grey clothes, her feet were bare and her flesh had a faint blue sheen.

'Help me – please help me.'

'I can and I will,' I said, going over to her, 'but this is not the place. You must follow me.'

The old churchyard led, through an opening in the far wall, to a more recent burial ground, with some twenty identical gravestones, little worn or touched by the moss and lichen. I had discovered that the hospital had taken over the space for the burials of patients whose identities were unknown of whom there used to be many more than there are now. I led the way to two of the graves, marked simply John and Grace above a date and a simple cross.

She was standing beside the entrance and I beckoned to her. She said again, 'Help me, please help me,' in that old, croaking voice, her eyes vacant. I still shuddered to hear it as I looked at her beautiful

257

face. Then, with steps that seemed hardly to touch the ground, she came close to me and as she did so, and for the first time, I smelled the smell of death and decay upon her. I did not shrink back. She approached the grave marked John and at once recoiled. I edged closer, speaking to her as reassuringly as I would to a child. I thought that I now understood what was wrong, though I was working more or less on blind instinct and I had a notion of how she might find her rest and resolution at last. She turned to me, looking fearful.

'No,' I said, speaking in as quiet and reassuring voice as I could. 'There is nothing for you to be frightened of. In this grave is the body of the old man whose life you were given. I can explain it no more clearly – it is beyond my understanding.'

She bent to read the inscription and I saw her whole being begin to tremble as she reached out her hand, as if to trace the outline of the lettering. I moved slowly along to the grave marked Grace and stopped beside it and as I did so I felt that same deathly chill wrap me round. She was standing very close to me and it seemed as if her breath was becoming fainter. The cold grew more intense. I was afraid myself now and felt unreal, as if I was standing beside my own body but I managed to speak, though it was hard and I could only get out a few words. 'Grace. Find. Go.' My chest seemed to be tightening and my throat about to close up.

'Back. Give. Back.' I could say no more. My brain was working slowly, in flashes of consciousness between terrible stretches of darkness. I knew what she must do, and that I was trying to help her as she had begged me. She took a couple of steps forwards. I did not see her turn again and now she was beside John's grave. I stared. Nothing happened and the bitter cold was binding me with iron bands now and the constriction in my chest was agonisingly painful. She glanced once more at her 'own' grave and I saw intense suffering and distress in her face, before she took a single further step, so that now she was standing right on the burial place. And then she had gone. She was no longer there. Nothing was there. At once, the chill that had held me lifted, and the pain and constriction were loosed.

I came to, as if I had woken from sleep but not from any dreams. I was fully conscious of where I was and of everything that had happened. Whatever help Grace had needed, I felt sure I had given it to her but I could do no more and I made my way towards the passage. The clouds had almost cleared and the moon shone with a soft hazy light. I looked back. Above the grave of John was a pale mist, not visible in any other part of the churchyard. It had no form and there was no sense of 'presence'. It was like the mist that sometimes happens over the surface of water at dawn. As I looked, it began to dissolve and I felt an uneasy calm. Whatever I had done, whatever had happened, I believed that the young woman had now found her peace, and that both she and the old man were somehow whole and restored.

Six

At home, work and country life absorbed me again and although I cannot pretend that I forgot about what had happened or that my sleep was always untroubled, on the whole I was fairly at ease.

A year passed. We saw Laurie infrequently – he was rarely free from the hospital – and when we did meet, he and I never referred to what I had told him.

One bright, clear morning in October, I opened a letter addressed to me alone, in Laurie's hand, which was somewhat surprising but I told Eleanor I had been expecting some medical information from him and, because I had a sense of foreboding, I delayed opening it until I was alone.

My dear Hugh,
In haste, but I thought this might interest you. The

names caught my eye in the paper and remembering your strange stories, I looked at the records for the era at St Luke's of those two doctors you knew. As you remember, Powell and McAllister were arrested, charged and bailed on various dreadful suspicions. They were both dismissed from the hospital and subsequently struck off the medical register 'for behaviour in a manner so as to call the profession into disrepute'.

They were accused of gross misconduct in relation to the certification and preparation of deceased patients and the improper disposal of their remains but there must have been far more to it, none of which could be proved.

I confess that I doubted your tale until I came upon this and of course, I am sure you are not surprised to hear that I still believe parts of it to be entirely fanciful – you could never resist embellishing a good story, as I recall from boyhood! I wondered what had happened to Powell and McAllister – who I assumed must have been imprisoned for some years but later released. Such men often disappear abroad, where they do not find it as difficult as it should be to continue practising medicine. I asked frequently if any older members of the hospital medical staff recalled them and eventually

an eminent pathologist, sometime retired, raised an eyebrow and said that such things were best forgotten but then he added, 'Their bodies were washed up just a few days after they were released on bail. I performed the post mortems. As I recall, both of the stomachs were full of strychnine and their hands and arms were held together by chains.' I asked if he had suspected murder.

'Who knows? But for my money it was a clear case of joint suicide. They were unable to live with themselves any longer and the world was well rid of them.'

The case may not be closed in police files but I am inclined to take the pathologist's view. So there you have it – a melancholy little tale but I hope you're interested to hear the end of it.

I had always known that what Walter and Rafe were dabbling in was evil and dangerous and there was no doubt in my mind now that the pathologist was correct. They had taken their own lives out of shame, guilt and terror of what they had done. It would have led to worse. They had stopped themselves in the only certain way. I felt nothing but cold contempt for them. I like to think that I am a compassionate man but in this, my heart was hard.

Seven

Postscript

Here, the small book ends. When eventually I read it, after my stepfather's death, I presumed that there was no more to be added. Whatever the truth of his story that was it –'a story'. Many a writer has told a tale in the first person and his own voice, as if he is recounting real events but I was entertained by the way Hugh had done it, presumably as a diversion from the often humdrum life of a country doctor. Why he had chosen this particular topic on which to base his fiction I had no idea but it was as good as many others and makes for a creepy tale.

At least, that was what I thought when I received the little book. I read it, put it away on the shelf and forgot all about it.

Hugh died at the age of ninety-two, pretty well and in command of his faculties until almost the end, when he became confused and not always fully aware of us or his surroundings. I thought he had suffered a small stroke, though if so, it did not cause him any physical problems and he continued to read and write letters to old colleagues, to play chess, do *The Times* crossword and to enjoy visits from Toby and myself. Toby, having retired from the Army and married, bought a small farm only half an hour from Hugh and Eleanor. I continued to work in London at St Luke's, but I drove down to the country every other weekend, now that my parents were becoming increasingly frail.

My mother died a year before Hugh and of course, not only did he miss her greatly but he seemed to have a strong sense that he was nearing his own end. He stayed in the old house tended by two wonderful women from the village and the visiting nurse, and I then went down every week. Toby or Joy, his wife and their two daughters, visited almost every day. I think that Hugh was as content as he could be and always seemed sanguine and philosophical and quite often downright cheerful.

He still took a daily walk around the village and even a little further afield when the weather was mild.

He was well known and loved over a wide area, and often met with old patients and their descendants on his walks. They would stop their cars for a chat and frequently give him a lift home.

I was due to go down as usual for the weekend when, very late on a Thursday evening, I received an urgent phone call from Toby to tell me that Hugh was extremely ill. Mrs Barford had popped in to see him at half past three and he said he proposed going out for a last walk. It was early October, the sun had been shining all day and there was as yet no hint of winter frosts or chill winds. She had reminded him that it was dark by five now and that she would have his supper ready, as usual, for seven o'clock. She last saw him making his way across the garden, and through the gate which led to the orchard – a favourite walk of his. From the orchard, the path led to the church and he could then return home via the body of the village, in a circular walk.

He had not returned after well over an hour and by then it was quite dark. Mrs Barford had raised the alarm and within a few minutes several men from the village had formed a search party.

Hugh was found in the churchyard, lying on the grass among the older gravestones. It was clear that he had suffered a severe stroke. He was got home, the local doctor – Hugh had appointed him as his successor – had said that he was unlikely to live very much longer and might well suffer a second and fatal vascular incident at any time. He was to be kept at home and made comfortable – the hospital was twenty miles away and would be able to do nothing more for him. It would be a cruelty to take him there.

When I arrived, Hugh was semi-conscious, the left side of his face slightly contorted, which gave him a staring, vacant look, and I thought that he had been frightened. I imagine he felt the first symptoms and knew he was alone and might die out there. He could not speak and I sat with him, alternating with Toby, through that night. He drifted in and out of sleep and his expression did not change until just around dawn, when he struggled to sit up. I tried to settle him back comfortably again but he clawed at my hand and arm and I saw that there was a be-seeching look in his eyes. His mouth moving, a few inarticulate sounds came, gravelly and hoarse, but he was not able to form any words. I tried asking him to press my hand if he wanted a drink or was in any pain but he only clawed again, several times, each time more weakly, his eyes intent on my face, as if asking, asking. But asking what? It was more than distressing to be unable to understand or to help him and I felt only a great relief when, just after six o'clock in the morning, he gave a sigh, his face changed, flickered with something I can only describe as delight for a second and then his body relaxed and he breathed his last, quiet breath.

We had already decided to sell the house. Toby was very well settled as he was, and I did not have occasion to take it over – my life and work will always be in London. We disposed of the everyday contents but we went through all the objects of value, the pictures and books, dividing them between us and sending the remainder to a saleroom. Toby entrusted me with the task of going through Hugh's papers, most of which related to his lifetime as a doctor, and it was while doing so that I came upon the pages that follow, which I presume he had intended to form the last part of his book. They were written in Hugh's own hand, legible but wavering – indeed, towards the end the writing became a wild scrawl which confirmed to me that he had suffered from more than one stroke.

I found myself greatly upset and unnerved by what I read and I could not – cannot – take it easily or lightly, as I once could the original story. I cannot get them out of my mind. I cannot sleep for asking myself endless questions relating to the whole business, from its very beginning in the old lodgings in Printer's Devil Court. Without knowing about the subsequent events, about Hugh's last walk to the churchyard at dusk and then his final hours, and the fear I saw on his face during his last moments I would still have taken it all as a tale he had cooked up himself. But as I read the ending over and over again, I became racked with doubts, troubled in my mind, unable to resolve any of it to my satisfaction. I still cannot.

I am horribly afraid that I never will.

Hugh's Final Pages

I had long forgotten all about her. But perhaps nothing is ever truly forgotten, it simply lies dormant, waiting to be re-awakened. Certainly I had not thought of her – of any of it – for many years when I took my walk through our churchyard that late evening. It is a beautiful spot, bordering orchards and meadows, and the gentle hills beyond. This was the soft end to a mellow autumn day. In a couple of weeks it would be Harvest Festival, the service I have always tried to attend. It means a great deal to us in the country. So I was in a calm and unruffled mood when I unlatched the wooden gate. Eleanor is buried here. I do not hang about her grave in a melancholy way, but I like to visit from time to time, to talk to her, to remember. I have never felt the least troubled or afraid in this sacred place. Why would I?

I turned and I saw her. There was no mistaking the young woman and I knew her at once. Everything raced in towards me as an incoming tide. I had thought her to be at rest. I had thought I had done all I could to ensure it. But now here she was and I was not only struck as if by lightning with the shock of seeing her, I was also confused. Why was she here? How did she find me? Seeing me, she stretched out both her arms and I saw the old, distraught and beseeching expression in her eyes, on her face. I felt unsteady but I also felt a sense of dread. I did not want to see her here, I did not want to remember.

'Go. Please go,' I managed to say. 'Go back. You do not belong here. You are not welcome. Leave me in peace. Go home.'

But she came quickly across the grass, barely touching the ground, as before, still holding out her hands to me, pleading. 'I can do no more for you,' I said.

She stopped a few yards away from me and began to speak – or at least, she opened her mouth, her lips moved, framing a rush of desperate words. But no sound came. No sound at all. She went on and on, gesturing to me, touching her face, her mouth, showing me what I already understood. She was dumb. She had given the old man's voice back to him but she had never found her own again and she had been searching for it, and for me, all these years.

I began to shake violently and I fled from her, stumbled away, making as quickly as I could for the gate and my own orchard.

I looked back once, hoping not to see her but she was still there, as clear as day and now she seemed to have a faint glow of phosphorescence round her. She was still holding out her hands, pleading, pleading and I could not bear it. I did not know how, but then I knew I must try and help her, as I had helped her before and I stopped and called out, 'I will come back. I will come back.' And I will go, I will go back …

(Here, the writing peters out.)